MW00608334

Life As It's Lived

Life As It's Lived

JACK BOYD

Texas Tech University Press
1989

Volume 1 of the Cedar Gap Archives
Copyright 1989 by Texas Tech University Press

All rights reserved. No portion of this book may be reproduced in any form or by any means, including electronic storage and retrieval systems, except by explicit, prior written permission of the publisher.

Printed in the United States of America

This book was set in 10 on 13 Galliard and printed on acid-free paper that meets the guidelines for permanence and durability of the Committee on Production Guidelines for Book Longevity of the Council on Library Resources.⊗

Frontispiece by David Smith
Design by Joanna Hill

Library of Congress Cataloging-in-Publication Data

Boyd, Jack, 1932–
   Life as it's lived / Jack Boyd.
      p.   cm. — (Cedar Gap Archives ; v. 1)
   ISBN 0-89672-207-4
   1. Texas—Social life and customs—Humor.   I. Title.   II. Series: Boyd, Jack, 1932–
Cedar Gap archives ; v. 1.
F391.2.B68   1989
976.4—dc20   89-5160
                                                                                        CIP

Texas Tech University Press
Lubbock, Texas 79409-1037 USA

PREFACE

t's tricky writing about a dogfight. You could start with the snapping and snarling, and continue right on to the raw meat and triumph.

Or you could begin with the winner, then use flashbacks to show the developing interpersonal relationships of the two dogs.

Or it would be possible to give a believable biography of each dog, including motivation, parental influence, and the color of the glowering sky.

Or you could say, "Wow, lookit there! Ain't that somethin'!"

That's the problem with organizing a batch of newspaper columns: What direction should the batch take? Originally these columns were published on Saturdays in the Abilene *Reporter-News* as the "Cedar Gap Chronicles"—published, we might add, to overwhelming acclaim. Well, two postcards and a raspy, semiliterate, obscene phone call is pretty good acclaim. In Cedar Gap, Texas, it's considered overwhelming, although as I think about it . . .

Anyway, the 750-word columns have been gathered into loose-jointed chapters, separated by a few freestanding monoliths—rats, that automatic steam-powered thesaurus switched on again.

Probably the best thing to do is use the wow-lookit-there-ain't-

that-somethin' methodology of column gathering. That way, if anything goes haywire, I can just blame the editor at the *Reporter-News*,
the one with the raspy, semiliterate voice.

Raspy? Semiliter . . . Hmmmm.

Nah!

CONTENTS

Life As It's Lived

CEDAR GAP ARCHIVES

Vera Frudenberg and Luther Gravely
Archivists and series editors

CHAPTER 1

ALL THE GOOD PEOPLE

usty weeds along caliche roads.

The smell of mesquite burning in a fireplace on a frosty December evening.

The image of a bottom-heavy quail straining up and over a bramble-covered fence, the smell of marble raindrops on hot pavement, or the burlap-textured sounds of the easy conversation of longtime friends.

Such stimuli can never be perceived isolated from the people who appreciate them. As fine as such visions and smells are, no place or sensation is worth a farthing or a yen without its citizenry, although those same high-yen or multiple-farthing individuals can often be as much trial as treasure.

West Texas is a curious amalgam of exasperating trials and heart-stopping treasures, of hero and dingbat living side by each on some of the sorriest dirt ever scoured and blown over a prehistoric lake-bed. Fortunately, a race of people ideally suited by genetic mutation not only lives and thrives in the dusty, clear, hot, cold, windy, unpredictable weather of West Texas, but members of that race can find subtle beauty in the silky tail of a skunk surprised under a garage. Or humor worth repeating in a well going dry. Or even delight in the majesty of a blue norther they know will drop the temperature thirty degrees in thirty minutes when they're a forty-five minute walk from the heavy coat in the pickup.

Such are the people of Cedar Gap.

A noble breed, they live in or near Cedar Gap, a smallish town— only 256 inhabitants—on an east-west Main Street a few miles south of Abilene, just off the Tuscola-Lawn-San Antonio highway.

The word we prefer is *inventive*. In a small town, every situation requires a series of tiny adjustments, those cunning and shrewd fine-tunings of an event that keep peace in the town and enough frijoles on the table to allow someone with a surprise visitor to command, "Y'all stay for supper, now, ya hear? You're lookin' too weak to make it clear home." Events considered spectacular in a major metropolis are shrugged off in Cedar Gap with "Well, what else could we do?" Cedar Gapians manage their spectacular talent for improvisation without boasting. Actually, most of them have it without even knowing they have it. They think they're normal.

Lester Goodrich's New Hat

For instance, more than once, we've proven that, like beauty, age is in the eye of the beholder; what you've got is considered new until you get a newer one. Or until someone knocks the "new" off the item.

Everyone in the Palace Hotel and Cafe watched Stafford Higginbotham drive his new propane truck around the block three times looking for an isolated parking place. "Sure, I could park in front of the cafe, an' the next thing you know, somebody'd swing a tailgate around and scar the paint. That's a new truck."

"Hey, Hig, what're you gonna do when you gotta drive out into the shinnery an' gas up a pumpjack engine?"

Hig looked more nervous than normal. "I just don't know, boys, I just purely don't know what I'll do."

There's your problem; nobody wants the "new" to vanish.

Last September, Bubba Batey bought some new Oshkosh B'Gosh

overalls. Ferrell Epperson, Bubba's boss at the Highway Department, mumbled, "That boy's so afraid he'll grease up those new britches, he eases on an' off that Case tractor like a skunk tiptoein' through a henhouse." Ferrell shook his head. "He's so proud of them, he hasn't worked two good hours this week."

That day at lunch, Ferrell deliberately tilted a bottle of steak sauce all over one leg of Bubba's new overalls. "He'd have been till Christmas finishin' his job if I hadn't done somethin'."

Leonard Ply, a pig rancher from down near Bradshaw, has a twenty-year-old "new" deer rifle. And that's exactly how long it's been since Leonard shot anything because he won't get near a mesquite thicket or a barbed-wire fence for fear of scratching that rifle stock.

"Hey, Leonard, some of us'r' goin' lookin' for coyotes tonight. Wanta go along?"

"Where y'all goin'?"

"Up on the mesa by the po-leese transmitter."

"Naw, I don't guess so. I might mess up my new gun."

But the best example of backspin is Lester Goodrich's new hat. As long as I can remember, Lester's worn this same battered off-white Stetson. Or he did until one day last week when I watched the wind blow it into the spinning fanbelt of his pickup.

He glanced around furtively. Then, quick as summer lightning, he grabbed the tattered remains and drove out toward his place. The next day he was back, the hat exactly the same as always, with two dim oily spots near the front and a little gash on the crown.

He was more than a bit surprised when I asked him about his hat. He blushed, his mouth twitched, and he looked at the ground. "I'm truly sorry you saw that. I guess the secret's out."

I asked him what could be secret about a hat.

"Well, with a name like Goodrich ever'body thinks I got a little piece of the rubber fortune. I ain't, but it don't stop people thinkin'. You know what those boys in the Palace Cafe are like. If I was to get a new hat ever' couple of years, I'd never drink a peaceful cuppa coffee for the rest of my life.

"Anyway, about twenty years ago, I heard the Stetson people were goin' to quit makin' this particular hat, so I bought up six of them and stashed them in my barn. This is number three. I got three more to go."

I told him if that's a new hat, I'm the king of Tijuana. I pointed at the cut up near the crown and the sweat stains around the band.

"Yeah, well." He looked around to see if anybody was listening. "I fixed those last night by the light of a Coleman lantern. I got some machine oil and drew those little spots right where they were on the old hat. Then I rubbed some kerosene inside the ribbon like I'd sweat all over it, and finally I took my knife to the crown." He grinned at the only artwork he would ever produce. Then he frowned. "I'd be beholdin' to you not to mention this to the rest of the folks around here."

I asked what to do with any remaining Stetsons if he ran out of breath before he ran out of hats.

"I'm savin' one to be buried in. I don't want anybody lookin' in that coffin and sayin', 'He sure dressed pore to be a Goodrich heir.' I'd a fur piece rather they said, 'Well, lookee there, ol' Lester finally got hisself a new hat.'"

Your secret's safe with me, Lester. Besides, if the secret did get out, most people would just shrug and say, "That sounds about right. It's a whole lot like that time ol' Bill Gadsten found that snake in his . . . ," and then they would list some historically important soul who got out of another problem in a similar makeshifty, jury-rigged way.

Corinne's Dream Trip to Paris

Mind you, Cedar Gapians don't go around looking for a problem just so they can show off a solution. For most of them, it's a lot more fun sitting on a front porch with a glass of mint ice tea and down-playing their own role in some past spectacular.

But when a problem does come along, they're ready. Like the time Corinne Iverson, our beautician and owner of the Fontainebleau Beauty Spa, received an invitation to go to Paris to describe her speciality, *Corinne's Beauty Mudpack*, made from mesquite sap and pulverized caliche. Now, we're talking Paris, France, which for Corinne was a dream come true, even if it was for only a week.

She landed in Paris knowing not a single word outside of *oui* and *escargot*. "There was this *cute* taxi driver who talked with a kind of a gargle, and he didn't move his lips, forever like Stafford Higginbotham when he can't find his spit cup."

Corinne spent the first day in a minor coma from jet lag. "My Aunt Natie's thirty-year-old girdle has more snap than I had." Then came four long days in seminars, and four long nights pushing her chunky body around after a tour group, sampling wine and ogling naked ladies introduced by men wearing green tuxedos and white makeup. "I'll tell you what, I learned a lot of things, most of which aren't gonna make it west of Fort Worth."

Finally, on Friday, the time came for her thirty-minute lecture-demonstration, but unbeknownst to her, the mesquite sap-caliche mixture had undergone an ominous mutation.

"I don't know if it was sittin' for five days on a French windowsill, or flying at thirty-five thousand feet, or what, but it had a sickly little green scum on it. It reminded me forever of Luther Gravely's eyes comin' out of a two-week drunk.

"Anyway, they gave me this scrawny, ugly, hollow-eyed forty-year-old French model with a little black peach-fuzz mustache that made her look like a stomped-on prickly-pear pad. I figured, how much worse could she look, so I lathered on *Corinne's Beauty Mudpack*.

"I'd only gotten as far as a little doughnut-shaped patch around the woman's mouth when suddenly that *Beauty Pack* set up so fast it crackled. That scared me, so I stuck my thumbnail under one corner of the hard doughnut and pried up. You ever opened a can of cocoa with your thumbnail? That's the way it sounded when it popped off.

"The model screamed, and her eyes got watery. She grabbed for my hand-mirror, took one look, then leaped up and began screechin' and pointin' to her upper lip.

"Well, fifty women must have stampeded onto that little portable stage, and most of them were fat, beady-eyed women with black peach-fuzz mustaches just like the model had. And I mean *had*. Her upper lip was as smooth and pink as a spanked baby's bobo. She held up that little piece of caliche-colored cement, and it looked exactly like Mayor Yancy's briefcase that time he accidently Superglued it to his cat."

Corinne was scared. She thought she was being gang sued until a rail-thin man in a double-breasted pinstripe whispered, "I vill pay vataayver you vant for thees magic hair-take-away formula." She tried to explain that something had gone wrong, but if he'd come to Cedar Gap, she could get him all the mesquite and caliche he wanted, and he could roll his own.

Corinne had taken only two quart mayonnaise jars of the magic formula. When the fifty women heard that, they began screaming and digging into the two jars and slapping it on their arms and legs "and places you'd just simply not believe, I mean, places I'm not gonna explain, either." They shoved Corinne off the stage, ruining her only pair of Wal-Mart pantyhose and causing her to stomp out mad. She never returned to the beauty exhibition.

As soon as Corinne got back to Cedar Gap, she mixed up some more mesquite-caliche elixir. "But it won't turn green. You ever seen my Aunt Ethel's rhubarb pie? My mudpack in Paris looked just like that."

Somebody asked if she was going back to Paris.

"Not in this lifetime. On Saturday I went out to Fontainebleau to see the palace and get some ideas for redecorating my beauty spa. There's some nice gold-foil wallpaper up in Abilene, and I can draw some pretty good vines and grapes around the windows. But that's as close to France as I'll get—unless I die and you plant me at the foot of a mesquite tree, and then send the sap back as hair remover."

She sighed and smiled as she headed back to work her magic at the single chair in her Fontainebleau Beauty Spa. "I'd kinda like that. But it's the only way."

Pickin' Up Inventory

It is the only way—for Corinne. But life as it's lived in Cedar Gap encompasses a myriad of possibilities. For instance, although we don't have an authentic junk dealer, that doesn't mean you can go out to our landfill and cart off all sorts of treasures. Ornell Whapple took care of that commercial opportunity. What some people call junk, he calls inventory.

Ornell owns the Cedar Gap Feed and Lumber, our main agribusiness, but that's not the inventory we're talking about. The Feed and Lumber is actually just a front for laundering the profits from his main business, namely, "trading-up."

Trading-up, a singularly southern vocation, consists of swapping something worthless (a pocketknife with two broken blades) for something less worthless (a pocketknife with one broken blade). Properly structured, this sort of transaction can gnaw up an entire morning.

"Of course," Ornell explained, "ya gotta keep in mind your string of tradin' so you'll know how well you're doin'."

Example: If you've got a perfectly good '52 Dodge dump truck transmission leaning against your garage, you've got to have instant access to its history from the time you swapped a bucket of miscellaneous tractor parts for a windup clock out of a World War II fighter, and from there through your temporary ownership of a thirty-five-millimeter sound projector, a Cushman motor scooter, four Asian goats, and a motorless Cessna.

"I had a great string of inventory goin' that was up to three big ol' potted ficus trees, but those Asian goats stripped my whole ficus inventory. I traded the goats for the Cessna, but now I gotta start another string clear back to three dead ficuses."

Inspired trading-up requires the total recall of a Mafia CPA. You've got to know, to the stripped nut and the cracked brace, the condition and location of everything "in inventory" and to have the butter-lipped ability to compliment and put down at the same time. I happened to mention a four-slice toaster I'd found down in Brownwood.

"That it shinin' in your toolbox? Aw, son, son, you'll be gettin' a major slice of my best material for that sort of gem. Hmmm, if ya fold it just right, ya cain't hardly tell that the cord's frayed, and I'm sure that dent didn't hurt the workin' mechanism much. Boy, lookit how that paper-thin material shines up! Here, lemme get that little flake a rust off . . . oops, I think we can tighten up that ol' broken handle easy enough. Hmmm. Listen, I got a matched set of genuine plastic ficus-tree holders you really oughta take a look at."

Ornell and Sadie Whapple live a couple of miles west of town on five overgrown acres of brush and gullies. Actually, they live on half an acre. The rest is dedicated to Ornell's weed-covered inventory. Nine wheelless cars and pickups of various vintages squat on cinder blocks, surrounded by piles of tires and rims, none of which fit the nine vehicles. Four auto engines dangle from four twisted mesquite trees, and rumor has it one of them actually ran within the past decade.

Ornell reserves his back acre for the "delicate stock," meaning toilets, bathtubs, and one French bidet. "I ain't too sure what that is, but it'd make a truly fine birdbath. Course, I'd need a bit more'n a dented toaster. You still got that splittin' maul you bought a couple a years ago?" Total recall is a must for an inventory man.

Because most women take exception to their yards looking like Berlin during the siege, the phrase *domestic tranquility* relating to a married inventory man is self-contradictory. Obviously, *lying* is not a word swappers cotton to, but *edited reality* does tend to surface in domestic explanations.

I asked Ornell about his greatest day of swapping. His eyes misted over at the memory.

"I 'member it was a Monday, an' I started early with just a little ol' Swiss Army knife. By noon, I'd gone through an antique tricycle, a collection of barbed wire, two pocket watches, an' a load of spoiled oat straw." He sighed at the splendor. "That afternoon I traded up through a ticket to a Cowboys game, three ton of reclaimed bricks, an' a muley deer lease until by five o'clock I had a runnin' pickup with most of the windows still workin'." Ornell frowned sadly.

"I was chuggin' up onto the mesa to collect some split firewood I'd got in another deal when I discovered that ol' truck didn't have a sign of a brake. It took off backards an' looped off a hairpin curve, threw me out, an' smashed into a boulder. Burned on the spot."

I asked him what he told his wife about his day's work. "Same thing I told the tax people," he smirked. "That I lost the pocketknife."

That was fast thinking, which is a way of life for certain people. The fact that most Cedar Gapians aren't lawyers and prefer to think before they talk doesn't mean that everybody is always in total control. In fact, if we ever make up a *Dictionary of the Gapian Language*, under the entry for *impulsive* there'll be a picture of Donnie Sue Kingsbury.

Deputy Sheriff Donnie Sue

Donnie Sue's a little bitty thing with blond hair and a flash to her eyes that could control anything up to and including a Saigon riot. She grew up here, then went into law enforcement down on the border with a couple of small towns and finally joined the Border Patrol, where she earned the nickname Chainsaw.

"I guess I did get a little aggressive sometimes." Which was akin to saying that the Mongols liked to travel. She was the only linebacker our girls' basketball team ever had. I reminded her of that fast break she interrupted during a playoff game.

"Aw, all three of those girls healed up fine." I waited. "An' their coach and timekeeper were only in the hospital overnight." I waited some more. "Well, they didn't score, did they?"

Not for the rest of *that* game, they didn't.

Nor did the "coyote" guiding illegals across the Rio Grande. She broke his trigger finger, dislocated his shoulder, and was holding his head under water when her fellow officers pulled her off him.

That's when Donnie Sue realized she needed a quieter area. Like back home in Cedar Gap where people understand dedication.

However, her intensity sometimes carries over into less august crimes, and a week ago Thursday, Donnie Sue became immortal. In five highly textured minutes she totally dried out and rehabilitated an alcoholic wife-beater.

About once a year, Morton Barstow realizes he's over fifty and, in a lather of self-pity, chugalugs more bottles of low-voltage comfort than his scrawny, dyspeptic body can process. He then makes his second annual bonehead decision: he finds Ora, his squatty no-nonsense wife, and blames her for his being old.

True enough, he does shove her around a bit, but it also has to be said that on a pummeling scale of 1 to 10, Morton is a 2 and Ora is a 9.7. Throughout their "discussions," Ora's bun doesn't even throw a sprig, while Morton's emaciated body winds up with startling similarities to post-Grant Richmond.

Donnie Sue happened to be cruising past the Barstow home that night when she misjudged a shadow on a window shade as a man attacking a woman. She couldn't know that Morton was only holding up his hands to ward off an old hickory-handled niblick Ora keeps for killing snakes and reeducating Morton.

Then Donnie Sue misread a sticking doorknob for a locked door, forcing her to blow the hinges with four shots from her .44 Magnum.

Since Morton was already reeling from Ora's rabbit-punching and niblicking, not to mention two six-packs of cheap Mexican beer and the echo of the Magnum, it took all of six seconds for Donnie Sue to slam Morton against an antique organ, scrape him across a wall of Barstow family portraits, then stuff his head clear through their old Hide-a-Bed sofa.

Ora screamed and grabbed the phone to call the peace justice down toward Winters. Then she held the phone against Donnie Sue's beet-red ear.

"Donnie Sue? Honey, this is Edgar Allen Plymate in Winters, an' we've talked about this before. Now, you cain't—"

"*You toad slime!* Beatin' a helpless woman—you don't deserve to *LIVE!*"

"Donnie Sue! Sugar, what're you doin' right now?"

"E. A. , just lemme alone. I'm gonna take this Magnum, and this puke-bucket is gonna look like—"

"You cain't do that, baby. You 'member that rabid dog you had to kill?"

She hesitated. "Yeah, I remember. I missed him on the first shot, and blew off a leg. And the second shot, I hit him behind the shoulder, and guts and blood flew all over . . ."

Of course, Morton heard only Donnie Sue's half of the conversation. He assumed she was describing a drug runner or serial murderer who gave her trouble. But when she said, "I know all he did was run across the street in front of my car," Morton knew immediately Donnie Sue had made hogslop out of a jaywalker.

The vision of his body becoming repackageable in Zip-Lok Baggies caused Morton's stomach to reposition both six-packs and fourteen dollars worth of microwaved junk food untidily on Ora's new K-Mart braided rug.

He was also instantaneously stone-cold sober.

So was Donnie Sue. She and Ora worked out an ad hoc parole agreement for Morton that made the Siberian gulag look like an afternoon at Six Flags.

Morton's white-eyed re-creation of the events for the Palace Cafe regulars grew with each retelling. Now, Cedar Gap traffic slows to a congealed ooze whenever Donnie Sue's patrol car is nearby. Also, truancy is down, littering is nonexistent, and cussing has deteriorated to "What the Sam Hill!"

On the other hand, Donnie Sue is having some trouble getting dates.

Oh well, good with the bad. At least we're feeling safe. Very, very safe. Donnie Sue's back in town.

SATURDAY'S JOURNAL

WHEN THE BUS STOPS

ell, it's Saturday again in Cedar Gap, and although the Greyhound bus has been and gone, Vernon is still sitting, waiting, as if the big bus should come back and apologize.

Vernon Cormack owns a couple of sections of sorry land west of Cedar Gap. He's the third generation of Cormacks to work that twelve hundred acres. His son, named Jeremy but called Tad, might have been the fourth generation. But a couple of hours ago, the bus carried away that dream.

When Irene, his wife, died about ten years ago, Vernon had to give his boy the name Tad. "I kept seein' Irene in the kitchen, brushin' some hair out of her eyes and smilin' and callin' Jeremy. I just had to change his name."

Tad's as bright as the point on an old plow, which is part of the problem. "Tad don't work the land like my daddy and granddaddy did. I've seen my daddy walk back down a furrow to kick a ragged chunk of dirt that didn't plow clean. I know it's pore land, but it's our land, and I'm proud of it." Vernon shook his head sadly. "But all Tad does is type away on that computer I bought him."

Some kids can hold a lamb and you know they understand about sunsets and summer storms and killing your own chicken for Sunday's dinner. Tad's eyes never glistened when a cow dropped twin calves or a neighbor's cotton made big. Vernon's boy worked, and worked hard, but he just never had the spark.

This morning early, Vernon drove to the Gas-N-Git where the Greyhound stops when somebody hangs out the sign. Vernon was pretty thin-lipped as he pulled Tad's little dufflebag out of the toolbox on his pickup.

"You comin' back here after boot camp," Vernon asked, "or will ya go straight to your schoolin'?"

"I dunno, I suppose they'll give me some time off." Tad said and hesitated. "Dad, about the ranch. I'm sorry I won't be here to help with the cotton or the sunflower crop. You gonna be okay?"

Vernon waved his hand to dismiss the thought. He was fighting not to look too long at his son. "I can fry eggs an' pour Post Toasties. I'll make it." He had to look away. "Now, while you're down there in Pensacola, you watch out for snakes an' alligators, you hear me? I heard they're fierce . . . an' . . . ."

"I'll be fine, Dad. The navy's supposed to have a real good computer program. Maybe I can come back . . . sometime . . . and set up your books on a computer."

Vernon turned his head to hide his eyes. "A little ol' place like this one, I'll just stick with a pencil an' the ledger your mama bought."

"Dad." Tad looked at his shoes. "I'm sorry I didn't turn out to be a rancher."

"Look, boy, you got a life, an' right now it's lookin' at a bunch of the world. Me"—Vernon spread his hands—"I got a couple a sections a scrub cedar an' prickly pear, an' a place on the back section where my people are all buried. You can only see one little piece of the world at a time, an' this is the part I want to see. Irene would have wanted you to—" Suddenly his throat closed.

"Dad, look, I . . ." A silver bus slowed and pulled into the Gas-N-Git parking area. "I couldn't have done it without the computer you bought when you sold that bull. Listen, I, uh, I gotta go."

Vernon clenched his jaw against the rising tears. He stuck out his hand. Tad shook it, as if for the first time, then he stepped into the bus.

Suddenly, the boy leaped out of the bus and grabbed his father in an enormous hug, his head against his father's faded blue denim shirt. Vernon's arms circled his son, memories of both a baby and a wife surging through the leathery hands. Then Tad walked back to the bus.

Vernon is still on the apron of the Gas-N-Git. Everybody circles around him, leaving him alone until the sad settles. We'll talk to him in a little while, jolly him up, but right now he just needs some Texas wind to blow away his tears.

It's tough to say goodbye to a son and a way of life on the same day.

CHAPTER 2

THAT CROWD DOWN TO THE

PALACE CAFE

ike any living organism, a social unit must have a pumping heart, a place that processes life-sustaining material, then dispenses it to the proper areas. And we're not talking about barbecue or six-bean soup. We're talking about information. We're talking people and attitudes.

In Cedar Gap, that function is taken by the Palace Hotel and Cafe.

You might say it started back in 1902 when an obscure entrepreneur named D. C. Smythe built the Palace Hotel and Restaurant, a two-story frontier hostelry with ten rooms, twin paths out back, and enough gingerbread to refurbish New Orleans. The hotel stopped taking boarders in '34, and in the late forties the restaurant mutated into a "cafe." Regardless of its name, the Palace Cafe has been the principal gathering place for Cedar Gapians for decades. Knowing intuitively that a diffused society is a dead society, we've used the cafe's oilcloth-covered tables and squeaky counter stools as a focal point for that urban sprawl called Cedar Gap.

As with any living entity, what goes into a citizenry is pretty much what comes out. You can't keep lathering ideas and ideals onto a social group without those individuals coming to believe that theirs is not only the best but the only intelligent way of believing. Years of repeated group attitudes, conversational gambits, and good-hearted bantering will scratch a tattoo on anybody's subconscious, regardless of the mental agility of the scratchee.

That brings us to a few of the scratchers and their natural habitat, the Palace Hotel and Cafe.

Food 'n Love 'n Cedar Gap

We know it's a Saturday in Cedar Gap when the 4-H Bon Appetit Homemakers Club marches into the Palace Hotel and Cafe, pencils and notebooks at the ready. We don't even have to look to know that IdaLou Vanderburg will be immediately behind the girls, beady eyes and clenched jaws ready for life-giving instruction.

In addition to being chief cook at the Palace Cafe, IdaLou sponsors the BAHC. Every year, she brings about a dozen teenage girls down to the Cafe for a lesson in home economics. Actually, it's a lesson in common sense.

"Girls," she said, lining them up two deep at the six-stool counter, "you're not in Paris. You're not even in Waxahachie. This is Cedar Gap, and we've got rules about cooking that makes the basic difference between an ol' boy muttering 'not bad' and whispering 'marry me,' so pay attention."

We'd all heard the rules for so many years we could have done a sing-along.

"First, this is Texas, so fry everything. And always save the grease in a coffee can with one of those little plastic Frisbee tops."

It's been said there are things living at the bottom of IdaLou's Palace Cafe grease can that scientists believe died in the first ice age. On the other hand, her Dutch apple pie with a touch of grease in the crust will make you slap your grandma.

"The next rule: Make sure it's done, and then add two minutes. Anybody says 'just drive it by an' I'll cut off what I want' is either showing out or he's from San Francisco, and you know what I mean by that."

When IdaLou gets an order for a rare steak, she marches out of her cafe kitchen, pins the wretched orderer with her gimlet-eyed stare, and argues until he upgrades the order or leaves. On IdaLou's scale of cookery, *rare* means the charred places are closer to brown than black. As she's said almost daily, "If I wanted that steer to heal up, I'd a left him in the pasture."

"Now, girls, this is very important: Don't ever measure anything. Oh, you'll lose an occasional pot roast or carrot cake when you're starting, but the sooner you learn to glug syrup by ear or pinch up the exact right amount of pepper for your stew, just that quick you'll have an identifiable, personal food. Plus, there's no way some old biddy at a church picnic can sniff and ask for your recipe. Glugs and pinches are great theft preventers."

IdaLou's concept is that food is life, and life is love, and love is men and women getting along together. Therefore, the better the food, the better the loving.

"Okay, girls, this is THEEEE most important rule. You serve a man store-bread, and he'll turn on you like a biting sow. You want him happy and saying 'Sweetie' and 'Honey' and turning over his paycheck on Fridays, just make sure there's biscuits at every meal. And I don't mean those sorry whomp biscuits that you—"

"'Whomp' biscuits, Miz Vanderburg?"

"Sure, you hit a tube of 'em on the corner of your cabinet, they go 'whomp,' and then you peel off little greasy slices. Just squeeze up some sure-nuff scratch biscuits, bake 'em up about the size of a dry-land terrapin, and make sure you got both a bowl of cream gravy and a Mason jar of sorghum molasses, and you won't have no trouble taming a man."

The girls scribbled madly, but one looked up and frowned. "Miz Vanderburg, right now I'd like to get *rid* of a boy."

IdaLou smiled. "No problem, honey. Just fix him three dishes. First, make him a sandwich without any real meat in it—you know, like tuna salad or something else you'd only serve to a bunch of women having hot flashes. Second, make a side dish of boiled okra which looks like something that just dripped out of a bull's nose. Then give him either cold coffee or warm beer."

"That'll make him leave, for sure?"

"Oh, it won't be him leaving. It'll be his mama telling him if she ever sees him with such a sorry cook again, she'll skin him alive. A mama just naturally gets the stone-cold tremors at the vision of her boy starving to death."

Later, somebody asked IdaLou if feeding a boy like that always works.

"Always. Of course, the girl'll probably have to move to South Dakota to find another man, because within a month, ever'body between Texarkana and El Paso will know about her cooking. But it'll work!"

Oh, it will, it will.

Cody Cuttshaw's Big Break

Being a voting member of that makeshifty social club that meets irregularly at the Palace Cafe carries with it certain responsibilities. First, you have to have a keen eye for evaluation and a willingness to express your beliefs, and second . . . well, second, you have to understand fidelity and courage on the community level.

For instance, a few weeks ago, just before noon, Cody Cuttshaw got a call from a friend in Austin. Cody's the local boy who leads a part-time country-western group called the Side B Band. They've been organized—using that term in its loosest possible sense— about two years, and in that time they've played every two-bit honky-tonk and tin-roofed dance hall within three hundred miles.

They'd looked and hoped for The Big Break, which had proved as elusive as a double rainbow. Until that magic day just before noon.

Cody's friend was in the right agent's office when the news hit that Willie Nelson's warm-up act had played an integral part in a four-woman, seven-man, six-knife brawl in Nacogdoches. They wound up with a twentieth-century group record for stitches and stomped guitars, and were unavailable for Willie's concert in Odessa Friday night.

The agitated agent wondered if Cody's group could fill in "just for tonight." Those of us in the Palace Hotel and Cafe heard the shout through six walls and an accelerating diesel.

"I'll tell you what," Mayor Yancy McWhirter said, "Cody'd better get some sueage insurance. If he don't turn down that volume for those Odessa folks, he'll be up to his gizzard in deaf-people lawsuits."

Bertie Faye Hogg, our postmistress, nodded. "My eyes blur for a week after he plays at our Third Thursday Dances."

"Aw, that ain't his problem," Stafford Higginbotham said, slapping down his coffee mug for emphasis. "Have you ever listened close to those words he sings? There ain't hardly a Christian song amongst 'em!"

Alton Hudnott said, "Yeah, singin' about some guy's designs on some girl for later that night, and he never does come right out and say whether they're married or not. I don't want *my* daughter hearin' that."

"How old's your daughter now, Alton?"

"Just turned forty-two, and I flat don't want her hearin' that stuff."

Ferrell Epperson, who's spent a few too many hours next to the mufflers on the highway department's tractors, just shrugged. "I don't see as how it make a whole lot of difference what Cody sings about or how loud. You can only understand about every tenth word, if that."

"And the other nine words are illiterate." Vera Frudenburg, our beady-eyed third-grade teacher at the elementary school, clenched her blocky jaw. "For twenty-seven long years I've tried to teach proper English to this town, but I'll tell you what, literacy rolled off that Cody Cuttshaw like clabber off rotten milk."

The crowd in the Palace Cafe kept growing, and every new addition had to stick an oar in Cody's already-muddy water.

"Why cain't Cody just stand up there and sing? He makes Elvis look arthritic."

"He's gotta move, 'cause if he don't, those tight Levi's will cut off all the circulation in his legs for sure."

"Well, he's got my permission to move around a lot more. That's the only thing that'll distract me from his sorry voice. I've killed shoats that made purtier sounds than him singin' 'Lucille'."

"Listen, I can take him singin' off the note if he'd just do some classics, like 'Walkin' the Floor Over You' or some real good Eddy Arnold."

Suddenly Yancy stood up, stretched, and sighed. "I'm truly enjoyin' this, but I guess we better get organized. How many's goin' to Odessa?"

Every hand shot up.

"Okay. Go check your streets and be back here in thirty minutes. We gotta order the school buses."

That's why the next morning everybody in Cedar Gap who was ambulatory looked like forty miles of Arkansas firebreak. Almost 150 people traveled in two school buses, six vans, and a hosed-down hay truck with folding chairs clear to Odessa to cheer on Cody Cuttshaw and the Side B Band when they opened for Willie.

I asked Yancy how many of the people poor-mouthing Cody went along.

"Ever' one of 'em, a course." I must have looked surprised. "Aw, you know Cody. He's a lot like an egg-suckin' pup; you don't always like what he does, but you figure if you hang with him long enough, he'll get over it." Yancy shrugged. "Besides, he's *our* egg-suckin' pup. That makes a lot of difference."

Not just a *lot* of difference; it makes *all* the difference. The fact that the next morning half the town looked like it had been washed on a rock and thrown in a corner meant nothing at all, because now they could all say they'd seen Cody open for Willie.

We Lost Two More Good-uns

One of the harder things in Cedar Gap is to separate the people from the places. If you see someone occupying a particular niche for, say, twenty years, even if that person is off buying a loaf of bread or seeing about a flat tire, the place is still occupied by your imagination.

Couples are that way, and if there was ever a couple, it was Blanche and J. D. Wilcocks. But we buried Blanche Wilcocks last Sunday.

She's been on the way down for a year or more, but what wasn't expected was the reaction by her husband, a bent-over, angle-jointed, stiff-walking retired ranch hand in his late eighties named J. D.

J. D. took Blanche's dying bad. Tuesday morning, he slumped on the old pew in front of the Palace Hotel and Cafe. And he quit eating.

Everybody walking by smiled sympathetically at J. D.'s leathery grooved and grieving face. "What was it, sixty-three years you 'n Blanche was married?" somebody asked. A slight nod but nothing else. "Hey, J. D., how about you'n me gettin' one a them barbecue sandriches?" A trace of a frown, a faint shake of the head.

Wednesday noon we finally figured it: J. D. Wilcocks missed his wife more than words could describe, and he was determined to follow her.

Little bunches of people huddled all over town to talk. "Whyn't we just get Doc to prescribe some a them little blue 'n white 'vacation pills' Sybil Jorgenson uses sometimes?"

"How ya gonna get 'em down J. D.?"

"Well, we could hold him, an' then—"

"You want us to treat you that way when you're almost ninety?"

Three dozen meetings came up with three dozen wrong answers, but at four o'clock we found out that committees aren't always the best answer.

Howie Breedlow is a middlin'-sized fifth-grader with unpartable brown hair, muddy shoes, and a sadness to his eyes since a truck ran over his dog last week. He sidled up and sat himself very quietly on the opposite end of the scarred pew, away from J. D. The old man never moved. Without any fuss, Howie pulled a small framed picture out of his coat and propped it up between them. Satisfied, he sat back and stared at the sidewalk.

Thirty minutes passed, then an hour. Finally J. D. tilted his eyes over toward the picture. "That your dog?"

Howie nodded. "Yessir." J. D. looked away.

Thirty minutes later, J. D. cleared his throat. "Is he a good dog?"

"He was, yessir." Howie's face twisted a bit. "A diesel hit him last week."

J. D. nodded, but waited another half hour to ask, "Your dog have a name?"

"Yessir. Rimfire."

J. D. rolled the name around on his tongue a couple of time. He nodded slowly. "Good name for a dog." A long pause. "How long d'ja have him?"

Howie tilted the picture back for a clearer look. "My daddy said me an' Rimfire was pups together."

An hour passed. It was almost seven o'clock when J. D. pulled a small browntone picture from his denim jacket. "This here was Blanche." His lips had trouble forming her name. "Good woman. Tolerant woman."

"Tolerant?"

"She was tolerant of me, and I weren't easy." A hint of a smile pulled at one corner of the old man's mouth. "And she uz a good healer. Ever' time a horse rolled on me or I broke somethin', she could put it back pretty close to where it was before. Or she could make me laugh at the new way it looked." His eyes never left the picture. "Good woman."

They held up the two pictures together and looked back and forth.

"Yessir." Howie bit one lip to keep it from trembling. "And Rimfire was a good dog."

The two of them, the young and the old, the beginning and the end, sat back, lost in the eye of the mind.

About ten o'clock, Howie's mama brought two thick comforters made out of surplus Army blankets and wrapped them around the boy and the old man. To her everlasting credit, she neither scolded nor babied her son. She just wrapped him against the night.

All night long, a succession of pickups and cars parked across the street from the Palace Cafe as families took turns watching out for the two quiet, sad, thinking men slumped in opposite corners of the old pew.

About sunrise, J. D. stirred and peered at the boy. He glanced at the two pictures lying between them, then he stood up. The motion awakened Howie. "You Travis Breedlow's youngest?" Howie nodded sleepily. "The cafe's about to open," J.D. said. "You need an egg before school."

"Yessir." Howie stood and stretched. "At the very least, I need an egg."

Then both men smiled shyly, picked up their pictures, and went to breakfast in the Palace Cafe.

The Olitsons' New Baby Boy

Things other parts of the world take for granted can be serious stuff for the Palace Cafe crowd. Weather won't just occur; I mean, there'll be no weather at all without a thorough analysis of the problem by a minimum of a dozen people. Water wells that were ignored by coffee-filled cafe regulars have been known to go totally dry. And naming something? Even giving a name to a new coonhound is worth a couple of conversations. Something as important as a new baby can chew up an entire week's energy.

That was the problem the cafe crowd ran into when Buddy and Trish Olitson were slow naming their new baby boy. The baby was almost a week old and had been home for three days. That meant it was nudging right up to time for a name.

"I never heard of not bringin' a name home the same time as bringin' the kid home." Milo Shively, our crop-dusting pilot, grimaced at his Palace Cafe coffee. "It orta be a package deal."

Buddy and Trish are newcomers from Pittsburgh, and their viewpoint is just a tad skewed from life as it's lived in Cedar Gap. Among other things, their family has a tradition of naming any new baby on the eighth day. Some kind of Biblical background, they say.

But the eighth day came, and there was still no name.

Oliver Greenslope dropped in from his Drugs, Notions and Hardware store. "I got a couple a name-books in our notions department that'll give them some truly fine ideas."

"If I still had that ol' three-legged pet possum a mine," Carter Burkhalter muttered, "maybe I'd name him one a them sissy names in your books. What Buddy oughta do is use my granddaddy's name— Delbert Thetchel Burkhalter. There's power in that kinda name."

"Sounds like somebody with a beard and spats," Oliver huffed.

Jakub Mielczewski, Cedar Gap's nearest answer to a medieval monk, turned on his chrome stool at the counter. "Vladislav." Every head turned incredulously. "Is goot Polish name. Name of onkle in Krakow."

"You walk into the auction barn up in Abilene with that name, you'd better be ready to fight. Sorry, Jake, people might think he was a Communist."

"I know what I'd call him," Bubba Batey shouted. Bubba, who started life with his batteries just under half power, poured some peanuts in a Dr Pepper. "I'd call him Lil Goober, 'cause he ain't bigger'n a peanut." A few people thought about that one, but since it came from a man who named his two half-breed hounds Hawk and Spit, nobody thought too long.

Lester Goodrich held up his hand. "Like any good Texan, Buddy oughta name his boy after hisself."

"Sure, call him Buddy Boy. That'd work."

"Naw, we already got us one a them over near Potosi. Now if it uz a girl, there's no end a fine names we could come up with."

"Like?"

"Loretta." Lester pronounced it "LOW-retta." "There's LOW-retta Lynn an' LOW-retta Young. Low-retta's a great name."

"Whoa! There's Buddy now. Hey, Buddy! Come sit. With ever' boy child, you get a free cuppa coffee."

Buddy's round face forced a tired smile. Old heads around the table nodded sagely. "Ain't sleepin' through the night yet, is he, Buddy?"

Buddy shook his head and sighed. "We've only had him home three days. Maybe tonight's the night."

"Uh, you decided yet what you'll call him?"

"Well, that's why I'm here," Buddy said slowly. "I think I told you that both Trish and I are second-generation American Swedes, so we decided to go back and use the names of our Swedish grandfathers."

You could slice the tension in the Palace Cafe. This opened up huge fields of arcane possibilities. To the cafe regulars, *foreign* meant anything beyond Texarkana, and Sweden was thirty miles to the left of the moon.

Buddy smiled as he lifted his cup of coffee. "Ladies and gentlemen, I give you my heir apparent"—he paused dramatically—"Lars Gustav Olitson."

Tomblike silence followed the announcement. People nodded faintly as they peered off into the distance. A few muttered the names singly or in tandem, trying them on for both size and resonance. "Yeah," somebody said, "those'll prob'ly do." A female voice said, "You and Trish done good, Buddy."

"One good thing," Milo said, "it'll cut down on potential confusion, 'cause it's for sure we ain't had any Lars or Gustavs around here for a fair number a years."

"Well, listen, guys," Buddy said hurriedly, "I better get back to my family. I just wanted you to know first."

"Yeah, take care, Buddy." "Tell the missus hey." "Call if you need us." "Don't lose too much sleep, now, ya hear me?"

The slam of the Palace Cafe door echoed through the silent throng. Corinne Iverson took a slow, deep breath. "Lars Gustav Olitson. It's kinda nice." She sipped her coffee. "But what d'you think it'll *really* be?"

Milo shrugged. "Either Butch or Buster, acourse."

Everybody nodded. "Sounds right." "Only way." "Goooood names!"

SATURDAY'S JOURNAL

GOIN' HOME TO THE GAP

e knew it was Saturday back down in Cedar Gap. Boy, did he know that!

She nodded curtly and assured him it was Saturday all over the state and the nation, and in fact, it was Saturday in the entire Western Hemisphere.

No, he insisted, it was sometime between Friday quittin' time and Sunday church in those other places, but in Cedar Gap, it was *Saturday*!

She stretched wearily and started to argue, but he nodded at a sign and yelped something about almost being home. She pointed out the fact that Dalhart was still four hundred miles from Cedar Gap.

For a long time, she stared silently at a brown landscape totally unlike her Idaho home. She wondered aloud about the value of reminding a town of its inadequacies by calling it Plainview.

He assured her they had an easy downhill shot from here! Straight south, a little jig east, then into Cedar Gap. Can't wait! They'd pull up in front of the Palace Cafe and they'd—

Her shaking head silenced him. She remarked on their two-year marriage, and reminded him that this place in Texas was not only smaller but had infinitely fewer possibilities than her town in Idaho.

He turned, smiled, and absolutely guaranteed her his hometown would accept her, and besides, he'd find a job pretty quick because he'd already written, and—

She cut him off with a reminder of the possibilities he'd left in Idaho, but he suggested that the so-called dairy work he finally found consisted primarily of cow waste-product removal, and the stacking of the raw materials for potting soil was, how could he put it, "limiting." He hoped this ol' pickup could hold together as far as Cedar Gap, and . . . wow, she'd see . . . she'd see.

No, she declared morosely, she would not see. She closed her eyes as the pickup bent around a smooth curve where the off-ramp sign proposed Roscoe, but the big sign promised Sweetwater. No, she thought, there's no place for me . . . for us. Then, still frowning, she slept.

A slight bump awakened her. They were leaving some kind of city. He pointed to a sign and echoed it: Cedar Gap—five miles.

Just watch, he asserted. We'll pull up in front of the Palace Cafe, and then you'll—

She yelled at him to leave her out of this. She'd always been left out before, always in her life. Always. As long as she could remember. Idaho. Texas. Those other places. Whereever. She wanted to be in a place, where . . . where . . . never mind, she choked.

He called her by a couple of pet names, and promised her faithfully that she'd see, that this was home, and . . . she'd see.

Her fingernails bit into her palms as the old truck rattled up in front of an aging hotel and cafe named, somewhat inaccurately, after a palace. She wanted to run, to leave before the people could turn their backs. Like the other places. Suddenly her door jerked open.

"Hey, y'all," a booming voice called, "looky here. Ol' Fred done it! He said he'd come back here with a beautiful woman, an' for sure, he done it! Ma'am, I reckon you'd be Tina."

She stared, startled by the smiling eyes surrounding the pickup.

"Come on, now," a lady, a waitress by her apron, said smoothly. "Let Tina rest. It's a far piece from wherever it was Fred managed to find this nice-lookin' a lady."

"What she needs," an older woman said, "is some Palace Cafe coffee. I'll get the cups."

"Hey, y'all come on in, now. We been waitin' for two days, since we heard from your cousin that you was comin' back."

"Right! We'll unpack your stuff later. C'mon now, the owner of this fine establishment is requirin' that we affirm once again that her barbecued brisket is the best in Texas. Here, Tina, this chair squeaks less than the rest."

"Boy, Tina, you shore look good for makin' a trip with the likes a Fred."

"Now, Fred, we know you been livin' too easy a life, what with cool weather an' a pretty woman like this to hang around with. I just hope you still got a few calluses, 'cause you start work Monday over at the Potosi Gravel Works."

There were too many voices for her. Her husband, in a haze of happiness, turned and winked. She tried the coffee.

Maybe, just maybe, she thought, the people here will be . . .

CHAPTER 3

IF YA ABSOLUTELY GOTTA GO

TO SCHOOL, YOU'RE BETTER OFF

GOIN' HERE

istorical Aberration: Miss Beatrice

There's always been the odd citizen who leans back, purses his lips, sucks on a tooth, then extols the virtue of a diploma from the School of Hard Knocks. Which, as anyone who has tried that style of education will tell you, is so much sowsoap. A classroom with a hard-driving, dedicated teacher will teach you a lot more about just about everything than you can learn banging your head against impossible walls.

That's why Cedar Gap's forebears, experts in the unnecessary pain in bootstrap improvisation, started the Cedar Gap Elementary School. It began as a little one-room frame building, then about 1910 it was upgraded to a two-room concrete-block building with a belfry. Finally, back in the fifties, the current tan-brick palace appeared, with indoor plumbing, a combination cafeteria and auditorium, and—oh, the glory of it!—a separate room for each grade from kindergarten through fifth. The teachers thought they'd died and gone to south Taylor County to wait for the real heaven.

Over the years, teachers have come and gone, but certain

memories remain, much more vivid than the bug-speckled class pictures in the entrance-hall display case.

There was T. Milburn Fleck, the first male teacher and coach of everything, who looked paunchily academic in his plastic collar and Teddy Roosevelt glasses until one of his tiny players received a bad call at home plate. Then he would stride to the scene, polish his round glasses as he looked blankly into the near distance, and inquire as to the umpire's knowledge concerning recent scientific proof that cretinism and temporary blindness occurred primarily in men wearing blue suits.

Or Miss Caroline Pliggins, a stern specialist in English literature, who insisted that her second grade read *Beowulf* and *King Lear* with perfect pronunciation and turn-of-the-century arm-waving histrionics.

But one name tops them all. You've heard of historical aberrations called the Victorian Era and the Wilderness Wanderings? A lot of us here in town were part of a legendary epoch that's come to be called The Miss Beatrice Years.

In our memories there now abide Fleck and Pliggins, but the greatest of these is Miss Beatrice.

It all came back to us a few days ago, and while the Palace Hotel and Cafe jukebox still mutters Willie's and Merle's and Emmy Lou's latest hits, nobody in Cedar Gap is singing them. "The Anvil Chorus" and Schubert's "Serenade" have taken over.

First, that's pronounced "Be-AT-russ," with the hard push on the middle syllable. From the Great Depression until she retired about fifteen years ago, Miss Be-AT-russ Bedford taught music and art to several generations of reluctant Cedar Gap Elementary School kids. Forty years, as girl and woman, she force-fed Rembrandt's *Night Watch* and Beethoven's "Für Elise" down clenched and gagging preadolescent throats.

Her hypothesis stated that to facilitate the climb from the primordial slime, all students would learn to sing the finest of musical literature. Otherwise, we would be forever wedged into the evolutionary scale somewhere between Johnson grass and a carp.

There was none of this "Oh, What a Beautiful Morning" or "The Itsy-Bitsy Spider" foolishness.

"If you can sing 'I'm Looking Over a Four-Leafed Clover,' you can sing 'The Anvil Chorus'," she would chant, the flat of her tiny hand punctuating each agogic syllable, her five-feet-three frame angled menacingly.

Miss Beatrice retired unbowed but unfulfilled. By a sizable margin, Cedar Gapians still prefer old Hank Snow and new Dolly Parton to "The Hallelujah Chorus."

Then, a month ago, the Cedar Gap Elementary School music teacher took maternity leave, and only one trained option existed.

Beatrice Bedford is pushing eighty, but there's no moss between her toes. She tills a garden the size of a football field, plays piano for the Tuscola Rotary and the Lawn Civitan, and fills in at churches for forty miles around.

She walked into that first eight o'clock class like Patton crossing the Rhine. "We've got one month until our annual concert," she said, flinging dusty paperback music books at startled fifth-graders. "I stored these above the boys' locker room in 1958. Page twenty-seven is Anton Rubinstein's 'Welcome, Sweet Springtime.'" She rolled a chord on the piano. "Tomorrow we learn the 'Triumphal March' from *Aida*."

Since nobody thought to inform the kids the music was beyond them, they did as they were told: They learned Rubinstein and Mendelssohn and Purcell in two- and three-part harmony. In tune. Without a Texas dialect.

The doctrine of the separation of church and state took a severe pummeling as the "Baal Choruses" from *Elijah* echoed before school, solos from Handel's *Messiah* rang through lunch, and weary voices galumphed through Dvořák's *Biblical Songs* at after-school practices.

Last night, the old auditorium, marinated by decades of floor polish and jelly sandwiches, resembled a fragrant anthill as the whole town packed in to hear the newest edition of The Miss Beatrice Years.

Miss Beatrice Bedford, the pride of life glaring out of her heart-shaped face, strode onto the tiny stage like an old warrior allowed one last joust. Four measures of an intro, and sixty kids, scrubbed till they glowed, launched into a two-part setting of Schubert's "The Trout."

A congregational sigh oozed out of an audience caught in a web of memories. A bit of improvisational humming must have nudged up on stage, because when the song ended and the "wonderfuls" and "bravos" died, Miss Beatrice turned on the piano bench.

"And now," she commanded, "we'll *all* sing Schubert's great art song."

The choral sound started tentatively as rusty voices more used to cussing John Deeres and yelling at toddlers mushed through the stilted nineteenth-century vocabulary in Schubert's paean to a fish. But from there on out, it was young-uns sing, everybody sing, ending with the "Soldiers' Chorus" from *Faust* and Verdi's "Anvil Chorus," complete with four kids banging ball peen hammers on old Nash brake drums.

This morning, little knots of people stood on corners and in stores saying, "I thought I'd forgotten all those words, but . . ." or "Betcha don't remember that I had the solo on 'Danny Boy.'"

Some just wandered around whistling or humming.

For at least a day, "The Itsy-Bitsy Spider" was dead, smashed on Miss Beatrice's version of "The Anvil Chorus."

And Miss Beatrice? I just saw her out painting her storm windows.

Odd. She looked about nine feet tall.

Willow Wands and Copper Rods

Of course, everything in Cedar Gap Elementary isn't Socrates, Mozart, and Thomas Edison. Theory and history are excellent guides, but hands-on experience is the only way for truly learning some concepts, such as milking a cow or changing a pickup tire. And when you come to a concept that smacks just a tad of unscientific voodoo, then . . . well, then you've got to improvise.

Karen Buckaloe is from a place too small for a zip code up in the Panhandle, which is why she requested Cedar Gap Consolidated Elementary School for her practice teaching. Our six-room school and ninety-four students fit her just fine, thank you.

And except for one little habit, Karen is doing an outstanding job; she keeps pushing her seventeen third-graders into more hands-on experiences than Vera Frudenburg, her supervising teacher, can righteously handle.

"I can take Karen getting Leonard Ply to pen up one of his farrowing sows, so the children can watch the, ah, birthing process, but witchcraft in my classroom is something else."

It started when a third-grader's two-paragraph report on West Texas weather mentioned a water witch. As a modern teacher, Vera figured she needed to hew to the company line and debunk witching as a method for finding water.

Karen bristled. "If it's scientifically impossible, then we should refute it scientifically." Vera's blood chilled as Karen struck a finger-wiggling pose halfway between heroic and afflicted. "Tomorrow, we *experiment!*"

That night, while Karen made a strategic phone call, the seventeen kids talked to parents. And parents talked to other parents. For a *long* time.

Wednesday morning, against the squint-eyed but silent better judgment of Vera Frudenburg, Karen walked her Gang of Seventeen a quarter of a mile to an arid acre of gravel and prickly pear bordering the Cedar Gap Memorial Airport. Waiting for them were more than fifty curious, apprehensive, or irritated adults.

Karen glanced quickly at the crowd and then at the unpromising dirt. "Children, I have willow, apple, and peach wands, and two copper welding rods. We'll start here with the willow."

She angled across the rock-strewn surface, the Y-shaped willow wand bent in her upturned and clenched fists.

"There ain't no water around here," a man muttered. "It's as dry as my mother-in-law's toast."

A woman narrowed her eyes at Karen's slim form. "Tight jeans and voodoo. You can bet the ranch there's gonna be trouble over this."

Suddenly Karen stopped. "Watch the tip, children." As she moved forward, the willow wand bent relentlessly until it pointed directly at the rocky ground. "Mary Anne, put a stob here. And explain crosshatching."

"You're gonna checkerboard it," Mary Anne said proudly.

"Why do we do this, Petey?"

Petey jumped as if shot. "To, uh, uh, check to make, uh, sure we ain't, uh, *haven't* messed up our, uh, yeah, scientific method." Perspiration dribbled off his freckled cheeks.

"Anita, shall we use the apple or the copper?" A tiny beribboned head ducked shyly as a delicate finger pointed. "Rods? Good choice! Here we go, and follow closely."

As her gaggle of silent children approached the stick marking the willow's dip, the thin copper rods swung outward until they pointed directly away from each other. "Looks like the place. T. C., let's celebrate! Break out our signal rocket!" She scratched a match and sent a small bottle rocket sizzling high into the sky.

Two minutes later, a huge drilling rig rumbled onto the gravel and weeds. In fifteen minutes, the tower was in place and the drill bit spinning.

A teenage boy shoveled samplings from each two feet. "See that white layer? Children, that's caliche. Good to drive on, but no good for water." Karen kept up a constant chatter, detailing layer after layer of underground history. "Now, that red layer could—*look out!*" A spurt of dirty water splashed up around the drill stem. The adults ran forward, chattering like rain-riled chickens. The kids laughed as they scooped up mudballs.

What came out of Karen's scientific method was the only artesian well in the history of our county. It flows only about a quart a minute, but that's enough to fill a nice trough for deer and birds. The kids named it The Lagoon of the Happy Witches.

Later that day, Karen zipped through the Palace Hotel and Cafe for a Dr Pepper before heading back to the elementary school for some late-night work. Somebody asked where she learned her witching.

"My grandmother, Miz Ada Buckaloe, was the most delicate lady, best Sunday school teacher, *and* finest witcher in our county. *She* taught me."

"Does witchin' always work?"

"As Grandma Ada said, 'Luck only has to work a day at a time.'" Karen winked and split a grin that lit up the whole cafe. "And yesterday it worked."

Ah, science and luck. Now, there's your quality team!

The Educating of Ollie Bill

But some educational problems defy both science and luck. Sometimes the only solution is a sincere ignoring of the problem. In such cases, no education is the best teacher. That was Oliver Greenslope's method.

The other morning, Oliver walked in the Palace Hotel and Cafe and ordered coffee for everybody. When somebody asked what we were celebrating, Oliver just squinted and mumbled, "An education."

Oliver owns Greenslope's Drugs, Notions and Hardware. Two weeks ago his twelve-year-old grandson, Oliver William Greenslope, came for a visit.

Oliver sat nursing a cup of coffee and shaking his head. "Ollie Bill's a good boy, but I gotta tell you, he's as unhandy a kid as I've ever seen. We tried buildin' a simple wooden birdhouse, but he couldn't pound a nail I didn't start, an' you can just forget about usin' a handsaw or a brace 'n bit."

The boy's main problem was growing up in a rich Dallas suburb where his mama and daddy got him every kind of educational advantage available.

"Unfortunately, all those so-called educational advantages start when you push a button. When it comes to loosenin' a stuck bolt, Ollie Bill don't know diddly-squat." Suddenly, Oliver focused his eyes on something in the general direction of Cleveland. Without a word, he jumped in his truck and headed out of town.

That was Monday. Tuesday morning, Oliver pulled the frame and bent front wheel of a '54 Morrison bicycle out of his storage shed. "Ollie Bill, if you can get that thing apart, we might be able to make you a bicycle."

"What kind of tools should I use, Grandpa?"

"Whatever fits an' seems like a good idea. An' you might ask around if anybody else has any Morrison parts. I'll see you at supper."

Like a cricket on a griddle, Ollie Bill zipped in and out of every store and house in Cedar Gap. A rear wheel turned up at Beeler's

Fine Used Trucks and Tractors. A seat and a coaster brake were discovered behind Ambrosio Gonzales's repair shop.

By Wednesday at four o'clock, bits and pieces of four bicycles lay scattered all over Oliver's garage. At four-thirty Oliver hobbled in, a cast on his right wrist and a bandage covering his left thumb.

"I had a flat, an' the truck slipped. Doc said a couple a weeks in this cast should do it. I just can't grip anythin'."

"But, Grandpa, I gotta leave Sunday! What about my bicycle?"

"Tell you what, you get all the rest of those pieces apart, maybe I can talk you through puttin' them back together."

"I don't know *how* to put things together."

"First, you get 'em apart."

It was midnight when Oliver and his wife finally dragged Ollie Bill away from the greasy bicycles and cleaned him up with turpentine and solvent. But no two bicycle parts were still bolted together.

After breakfast, Oliver said, "That stack of parts is pretty confusin'. Sort out what looks good to you, an' I'll check 'em at lunch."

At noon, Oliver ran through the garage. "Sorry, Grandboy, I gotta drive to Abilene. While I'm gone, see if any parts fit into any other parts. I'll help after supper."

But that night he had a deacons' meeting. "That pedal looks great! Clean up that chain an' see if it'll fit the sprocket. See you in the mornin'."

All the next day, Oliver ran through his garage like a ricocheting bullet, apologizing and suggesting. Finally Oliver said, "You air up those tires, an' I think that bicycle of yours is about ready to run."

An hour later, a brown, red, gold, blue, and rust bicycle squeaked unsteadily toward Oliver's drugstore. Everybody applauded. Oliver beamed.

When I finally got Oliver off to himself, I told him I didn't remember even one of that particular brand of bicycle in town, much less four.

Oliver laughed as he began pulling apart the cast on his wrist. "Actually, I got those bicycles at four junkshops in Abilene. I dropped 'em off all over town with people I could trust. I put the handlebars in Zaccheus Tatum's henhouse and scattered chicken manure all over it to make it look like it'd been there a long time."

And the chain and sprocket?

"Same thing, only at Hig's place, and it was pig manure. Ooooooh, that's vile-smellin' stuff."

Why such nasty material?

"I knew Ollie Bill *said* he wanted a bicycle." Oliver's eyes squinted toward Cleveland again. "I just wanted to know if he really, I mean *really*, wanted a bicycle."

What do you reckon Ollie Bill learned?

"One thing was that fingers clenchin' around a screwdriver produces a truly fine feelin'." Oliver grinned. "And that time goes slower when you're pickin' pig manure out a bike chain with a mesquite thorn."

Oh, it does, it does.

Dick, Jane, Spot, and Russ

Every educational venture doesn't work out, but recently we watched Russell Underwood join the real world.

Russ took over Underwood's Septic Service when his daddy died. Russ was only fifteen and not doing well at all in school, so with a collective sigh of relief, the school allowed him to quit and go to work.

Four years later, he married Edie Loffland, and now their two kids, Davie and Anita, are in the third and first grades. The Underwoods appear to be an ideal family. Except Russ is illiterate, with all of the anguish and embarrassment that goes with that problem in the modern world.

Vera Frudenburg, our third-grade teacher, just shakes her head. "Russ was as good a kid as I've seen, but he couldn't read a word." That sort of failure gnaws at Vera. She takes it personally when she misses a kid. "It's good he works where reading doesn't matter."

Maybe it doesn't matter in septic tanks, but in the quiet times, to every human mind, reading matters greatly. We've all watched Russ, Edie, and the kids come in the Palace Cafe for a meal and turned our heads when Russ asked Davie to read the menu to him. Or we just nodded when he finished a job and then said, "It'll be easier if I bill you for this." We knew he couldn't write up a sales ticket. Even worse, he knew that we knew.

We've had people here in Cedar Gap who were unable to read, but it's been a bunch of years, and we're out of the habit of having them around. Russ feels this discomfort and does what he can to laugh it off. "Well, my kids are twice as smart as anybody in town, so I guess it all evens out."

Somehow, it never evened out in his face. Already, at thirty, lines had formed, his smile was pinched, his eyes beaten.

Then, about six months ago, Russ became scarce around town. He still did his cleaning work, but he never came into our poolhall at the back of the cafe or attended the open meetings of the town council. A little later, people began commenting on the strange set to Edie's jaw.

"Whattaya reckon, Russ's taken to drinkin' alone?"

"Nah, it ain't his style."

"Well, somethin's sure happened. Suppose one of 'em's sick?"

"Don't know. They're up a lot later'n they used to be. I pass right by their house, and their light's on pretty late."

Our concern lasted up until about an hour ago. Then, with the Palace Cafe filled with the midmorning crowd, all four of the Underwoods walked slowly through the front door, Edie leading, the two kids pulling Russ, who looked like he'd been told to swallow a rat.

Edie pushed Russ onto one of the two vacant stools at the counter, then took the other herself. Davie, the third grader, held onto Russ's left hand. Anita, pigtailed and ribboned like church day, hugged Russ's right arm.

The noise in the cafe dipped when the Underwoods walked in, but then everyone began making odd word and sentence choices just to push back the silence. Nobody looked at Russ, which meant *everybody* looked at Russ.

"Well, let's see, Russell," Edie said in a too-loud voice, "it's a little early for lunch, but we might have a snack. What do you see that you like?"

Ice caves in Antarctica are noisier than the Palace Cafe as we waited for the embarrassment of Russ asking Davie or Anita for some suggestion.

"Well, uh, I see they got . . . coffee . . . and, uh . . . I see they got, mmm, pie . . . and they got . . . bar . . . bee . . . cue . . . barbecue! sand . . . wiches." He turned to Edie, his face glistening with sweat and pride. "Anything sound good to you guys?"

I don't know who was more drenched with sweat, Russ or the cafe listeners. Mouths dropped, eyebrows shot up, heads swiveled.

Edie turned to her son. "Davie, give your father that copy of the *Galaxy-Telegraph* he asked for."

Russ's eyes widened as if to say, "I'm gonna die right here." But he took the paper, snapped it a couple of times, then peered at the front page. "Ah . . . ah . . . well, how about that, we're getting a new fire hy . . . drant down on . . . South Street." He licked his suddenly parched lips. "And it will only cost . . . six hundred . . . and forty-two dollars"—the crowd leaned into the sentence—". . . and twenty-five cents!" he finished triumphantly.

Russ got one of the few authentic standing ovations in the history of Cedar Gap. We hugged all four Underwoods, but particularly Edie because she was the one who took Davie's and Anita's schoolbooks and patiently spoon-fed Russell Underwood "survival reading."

He's not ready for Shakespeare or even the editorial page of the *Galaxy-Telegraph*. But Russell Underwood can read most of an election ballot and a hymnbook and his kids' report cards. Those are good starters.

See Russ read.

Read, Russ. Read!

SATURDAY'S JOURNAL

WORDS YOU WON'T NEVER HEAR

IN CEDAR GAP

ell, it's Saturday again in Cedar Gap, and we've been working on a few more entries in our *Dictionary of Basic Gapian*. Although English (or "Murrican," to use the vernacular) has a quarter of a million words or so, Cedar Gap gets along just fine, thank you, on a couple of thousand.

The rest of the 248,000 words might surface in Sunday school or other forms of stress, but several will never *ever* be used. Our dictionary not only defines those essential two thousand, it lists the ones never even considered. Words like *sushi* or *Christian Dior*.

The high-tech world is slow to filter into Cedar Gap. When bits and pieces of Crosley radios, Nash pickups and B-17s are still circulating in our trucks and combines, it's a tad presumptuous to get excited about Mitsubishis and Porsches (unless the Mitsubishi concerns a part off a bomber that went down on Guadalcanal).

A computer salesman dropped in on Murphy Gumpton across the street at the Cedar Gap Mercantile. Murph sells dry goods and small appliances at the Mercantile and still writes up tickets that use little bitty scraps of carbon paper.

"This computer, Mr. Gumpton, will eliminate all of that hand-work and tell you about inventory shrinkage when you—"

"Sounds like you're talkin' about stealin'."

"Ah . . . yes, that's a quaint way of describing it. All you do is interface this terminal with our main-frame operator in Omaha, and—"

"Inter-what?"

". . . mmmm . . . connect! Is that a good word for you? Our terminal lady in Omaha can pull down a menu that will—"

Murphy gently suggested that Mrs. Gumpton was far more qualified to check on the occasional lost frock or toaster than the lady in Omaha, who, if she is terminal, needs bed rest more than a telephone call from Mrs. Gumpton, although Mrs. Gumpton's Hospital Visitation Group from down at the Baptist Church would be happy to drop a card to the unfortunate Omaha lady. Murph helped the salesman interface with his station wagon before checking out the only menu that appealed to him, the leatherette one over at the Palace Cafe.

In our *Dictionary of Basic Gapian*, under the entry "Don't even think about these words," are two current favorites—*vulnerable* and *sensitive*.

"When I add a word to my vocabulary," Carter Burkhalter snorted, "I try to imagine John Wayne or Willie Nelson usin' it in a sentence."

Arnold Curnutt leaned into the conversation. "Can you imagine the Duke cornerin' a bunch of smelly, tobacco-stained outlaws an' sayin', 'Uh, guys, when you ran off my cattle and shot my daddy, it made me feel a bit, you know, like *vulnerable*' "?

Carter slapped the table. "That's exactly what I mean. I just can't see Dirty Harry's boss askin' him why he blew up fourteen Ay-rab terrorists, an' Harry whisperin' that he was just tryin' to get in touch with his feelin's."

Even Luther Gravely, our resident psychologist and inebriate, listened to some drive-through visitor talking in the Palace Cafe. The visitor kept saying, "I'm just traveling around trying to find out who I am. I mean, really, who *am* I?"

Luther dribbled his homemade vacation juice in the stranger's coffee until the man passed out. Then Luther carried the stranger out to his car, ripped open the man's shirt, and with a Magic Marker printed the man's name on his chest with an arrow pointing straight up his throat and circling his ear. We asked Luther if he counted the stranger a full cure, or was it only a temporary patch job.

"He didn't come back, did he? Musta figured out who he is an' called home. I shoulda charged him. I mean, world-class psychiatric help is tough to find on short notice."

Of course, sometimes minimalism is the best bet. Monroe Sternly, our crotchety bachelor, slumped into the Palace Cafe for coffee. Brenda Beth, the owner and our best waitress, walked over. "Mornin', Monroe."

"Mornin'."

"Coffee?" she asked.

"Black."

"Barbecue?"

Monroe nodded.

"Bowl or plate?"

"Plate."

"Rain at your place?"

He thought about it, nodded, then got up and walked to the far corner of the cafe. Somebody asked if he was mad at something.

"Nope. Just can't stand a talkative waitress."

Monroe doesn't need even the full two thousand words. About 170, plus facial twitches, suits him far better.

CHAPTER 4

BUBBA BATEY AND

THE ECOLOGICAL BALANCE

eeping That Tricky Balance

It was a pure joy recently to watch Sybil Jorgenson floorboard her '47 Studebaker all the way back to her rock house on South Street. Sybil was no longer a pedestrian. "Ambrosio's done it again," Leonard Ply mumbled and shook his head.

True enough. Ambrosio Gonzales, a Mexican mechanic of unparalleled intuitive genius, manages to keep our county's ancient vehicles and farm implements running when other mechanics give up in disgust. Sybil's Studebaker is just one of our more visible examples of his instinctive creativity.

"Heard a collector over in Weatherford offered Sybil any new car she wanted in swap for that old Steady-breaker." Leonard yanked his tan twill pants up past his potbelly.

Lester Goodrich gasped for breath after sprinting out of Sybil's trajectory. "I doubt that collector knows that Ambrosio's grafted bits and pieces of everything from John Deeres to Cessnas onto that car."

"How's that different from that ol' Ford pickup of yours? Where'd you say Brosie got that carburetor he put on it?"

"Aw, you know, off 'n that funny little Kraut car somebody totaled down near Lawn. Forty-year-old trucks are tricky."

Which is the story of Cedar Gap. Little towns are as tricky as old cars and trucks. Occasionally you have to improvise to keep them going.

Somewhere, Lester came up with the term *ecological balance*. "You know, one year we'll be up to our galluses in jackrabbits, so purty soon here come the coyotes. Next thing you know, the jacks are gone, an' a week later, so are all the coyotes. Ecological balance."

Of course, once in a while there's a severe need to nudge your thumb up under the ecological scale to get a true balance. And that brings us to Delroy "Bubba" Batey.

When Bubba began this marble game we call life, he started several yards behind the taw line with only peewees for shooters.

"I've never known whether it was inherent local kindness or teacher burnout that got Bubba Batey through the sixth grade," the school principal said, "but the only time that boy'll rise higher will be at the Second Coming."

A town totaling 256 people can only tolerate one drone, and as our area inebriate, Luther "20-20" Gravely's stob is firmly in that slot. Fortunately, Luther's master's degree in psychology provided him a debilitating symptom his pride could live with, so when Bubba showed up with too much slack in his kite string, the town had a severe problem: Bubba had to go to work. But doing what?

The summer Bubba turned sixteen, four men quietly cornered Luther Gravely to explain life and basic survival in explicit, nonnegotiable terms.

"To keep your place among the idle poor, Luther, you're gonna borrow the highway department's Case tractor ever' night an' teach Bubba Batey to drive it well enough to pass the highway mower's test."

Picture it: a psychotic alcoholic guiding a frantic, benign thickwit through the intricacies of a four-speed transmission on a dark, rocky, rattlesnake- and scorpion-infested hillside.

For six weeks, Bubba threw chunks of limestone the size of cantaloupe all over south Taylor County as he sweated under Luther's profane and headache-ridden tutelage. Bubba lumbered through his nocturnal classwork, urged on by a screamed alcoholic vocabulary containing more variations on unnatural human interaction than he dreamed existed.

But Delroy "Bubba" Batey learned to drive that Case tractor better than anyone in the history of the Taylor County Highway Division. What Larry Bird could do with a basketball, Bubba could do with that Case. As a side benefit, all of those high-intensity night classes out on that rocky hillside gave a spectacular adjectival glitter to Bubba's otherwise bland vocabulary.

Bubba passed the test with a record score, and the Cedar Gap civic balance was back level. The local highway department's road crew got an excellent hired hand who worked long hours with neither a complaint nor an original thought, ideal attributes for a professional road trimmer.

An hour after Bubba got the job, Luther inaugurated a two-week alcoholic coma, during which he came forward three times on the same Sunday night at the Baptist Church. Luther wasn't repentant, just grateful for surviving the rattlesnakes and flying rocks of Bubba's vocational apprenticeship.

Nobody ever found out who the four men were who arranged Bubba's tuition. It didn't really matter. Somebody would have done it. In Cedar Gap, you just naturally do what has to be done to keep the balance, and balancing Bubba is generally looked on as a more or less full-time community project.

Ol' Bubba's Ecology Stuff

Since Bubba was born about half a bubble off plumb, this mental tilt sometimes causes his reach to exceed his grasp. Such a penchant makes him a natural target for some innocent jokes. Like the time Waldo Beeler hid a newborn puppy under a setting hen, then pulled it and some broken eggshells out and showed them to Bubba. "Musta just hatched. Whattaya think, Bubba?"

"Well, I know one thing for sure," Bubba said, turning green, "I've et my last egg."

As a tractor mower for the highway department, Bubba gets a lot of time to think. Far, far too much time. The problem is, the only things he thinks about are the last words said to him before he revved up his tractor.

There's been a push to save money at the highway department. Last Monday, the road crew was coffeeing up before starting out when Ferrell Epperson, the district supervisor, said, "I hear tell Iowa's usin' some of its surplus corn to make alcohol, and then burnin' it in their state vehicles. We oughta give that a try sometime."

Bubba's mind is like the grill on the front of Sybil Jorgenson's old Studebaker: it'll filter out birds and clods, but some indiscriminate grit is going to get through. All Bubba retained was "alcohol" and "try it."

All day Monday, those words bounced and scratched in the echoing void of Bubba's mind. The muttering engine seemed to say, "Try-it-try-it-try-it." When he downshifted, the grinding gears clanked, "Alcohol-alcohol."

Late that night, he shook a comatose Luther Gravely, who lay snoring his way out of a liquid celebration of the birthday of schizophrenia. Despite his master's degree in psychology, Luther's main occupation is medicating a mild battle fatigue with his own homemade elixir. "Hey, 20–20, I need a gallon of your cough syrup."

"Naw, ya don'." Luther belched. "Isss too strong fur boys." Then he fell back into his slack-jawed stupor.

"Ain't neither," Bubba whispered. He rummaged quietly through Luther's closet until he found a gallon jug of sweet-smelling liquid.

Twenty minutes later, Bubba pulled his old Case tractor halfway up the dark, moonless hillside beyond the Memorial Airport. He licked his lips nervously as he poured Luther's vacation juice into the gas tank, which was almost empty. Then he pushed the starter switch and stepped back.

It took about a minute for the chugging engine to burn the gasoline in the fuel line. Suddenly, the undiluted home brew hit the hot pistons.

A deafening backfire blew the tractor's muffler spinning into the night sky as it jarred the transmission into gear. A streak of flame like an enormous blowtorch roared out of the gaping muffler's hole, almost but not quite drowning out Bubba's terrified screeching.

Like some primordial fire-breathing beast, the driverless tractor plowed resolutely through a thick stand of shinnery and a ditch full of pecan saplings. It hit the airport fence full out, snapping cedar posts and sending rusty wire screaming through staples for two hundred yards in both directions. The unguided missile was fifty feet from Milo Shively's crop-duster hangar when the white-hot carburetor exploded. Shrapnel dropped on houses all over Cedar Gap.

Other than his pride, Bubba's only injuries came as he stumbled through the dark night, tripping on shinnery stubble, dodging flying mower debris, and screaming futilely at the careening tractor.

By Wednesday afternoon, the Future Farmers Club had the airport's wire fence repaired. Ambrosio Gonzales towed the smoking tractor to his Old Chihuahua Repair Shop and by yesterday actually had it running. "I use a carburetor I theenk come from thees '37 LaSalle," he explained softly.

As I said, the physical damage was limited, but the injury to Bubba's self-esteem was almost terminal. He's been looking like the little end of nothing shaved down to a fine point until just this morning when we finally got him over to the Palace Cafe for four cups of Brenda Beth's coffee and lots of bragging about his Texas-sized initiative.

Bubba stretched and smirked. "Well, at least Ferrell said I wasn't fired. But I'll tell you what, sometimes life's like cowboy dancin' with a fat girl." We waited and held our breaths while he took a slow drink of coffee. He looked up. "Aw, you know. Ever'thin' you can see is movin' in three different directions . . . and you ain't got no control over any of it."

Château Bubba's Heady Bouquet

But even for Delroy "Bubba" Batey, some things work out. Or nearly so. Like the time he almost become Baron Batey of Wine Fame.

One Monday, Bubba was mowing an isolated ravine when a man suddenly bolted from a thick patch of cedar and leaped wildly down the mesa. Just then, Deputy Sheriff Donnie Sue Kingsbury led a bouncing posse of three four-wheel-drive cars with sheriff's stars and flashing lights as they roared across Bubba's ravine in hot pursuit of the sprinting man.

Bubba frowned, then sniffed. A smell of something sweet and tangy, like his mother's berry jam cooking, drifted down the hillside. He thought about it a while—a common enough procedure for anything more complicated than combing his hair—then picked his way through prickly pear and mesquite until he found a crude, low-roofed lean-to snuggled up against the mesa.

Rough boards framed the entrance to a low cave, and nestled against the cave's walls, dozens and dozens of gallon jugs gurgled merrily. In one corner, a gas hotplate flickered under a large copper coil.

Bubba glanced around furtively, then sniffed one of the jugs. "Smells like Luther," he whispered. "Must be wine!"

He grabbed the two nearest jugs and galumphed to his mower. He stowed them in his equipment box, then ran back to the cave. The gleaming jugs so mesmerized Bubba that he didn't notice the thin copper tube running across the doorway. His boot caught the tube, yanking it up. A hissing noise and a smell like rotten onions galvanized him. "Propane!" he choked.

Bubba spun and lunged for the door. A second later, a spark from the burner caught the spewing propane. The explosion's shock wave shoved Bubba boots-over-appetite down the rocky hillside. Glass shards from broken jugs zinged through mesquite limbs like bird shot.

As he staggered to his feet, he saw in the distance the flashing red and blue lights of Donnie Sue's posse spin in a cloud of dust and head his way.

After Donnie Sue certified that Bubba was fine—she never revealed her benchmark for evaluating—she told Bubba to follow her on his tractor as she roared back to the Palace Cafe.

"Bubba's the hero today!" she said proudly. "He found that still we been lookin' for for a month. The guy was makin' brandy by distillin' homemade wine." Donnie Sue shook her head sadly. "Unfortunately, it musta been booby-trapped, 'cause none a the evidence survived."

You have to remember that Bubba was born about two sandwiches shy of a picnic. His mind raced, which means a slow idle to most people but fierce effort for Bubba. He was about to mention the two jugs, but Donnie Sue headed for the door. "I gotta get my report in. Thanks again, Bubba. I'll mention your name."

Bubba nodded carefully, his head still ringing from the explosion. He waited while the congratulations and stories of former moonshiners died down, then he walked stiffly to his tractor and carried in the two warm, dusty jugs.

The cafe's noise level dropped to zero. "That what I think it is, Bubba?" somebody asked.

Bubba nodded painfully. "I didn't know whether I should bring it out an' show it to Donnie Sue or not. Whattaya think?"

"Well," Carter Burkhalter said carefully. "The first thing to do is determine whether or not it's what Donnie Sue said it was. No sense in gettin' her hopes up about useless evidence. Right, guys?" The crowd gave a chorus of curious *yeahs* and *rights* and *you bets*. "Whyn't you get us some glasses, Brenda Beth?"

Luther Gravely sidled over. "It's a good thing you got at least one expert in this town."

Bubba splashed an inch or so of the purple liquid in several glasses, but Luther grabbed the other jug, yelled, "Ladies and gentlemen, I give you Château Bubba!" and knocked back several lengthy glugs. The rest of the cafe squinted, then sipped at their glasses. Suddenly, everyone coughed, two leaped for the back door, and Carter lost his breakfast and lunch in the potted palm.

Slowly the coughing and gagging subsided. The only sound was Luther muttering as he squinted at the jug.

"Ah, it's a saucy little vintage, muscular without being domineering." He took another long slug. "Yep, Château Bubba's a heady brew, although still an adolescent for sure." Another ten-second swallow. "It has a fine nose, a vague but definite bouquet of roses. Possibly if it breathed a bit . . . Naw, better get it young and brisk." He walked unsteadily toward the front door. "Actually, more scientific study is needed before we turn state's evidence."

Somebody started to object to losing half of the evidence, but Brenda Beth held up her hand. "Best leave him be," she said quietly. "Château Bubba's only for proven warriors, not for us civilians."

True enough, there's room for only one samurai in this town. As variations on the story began circulating, no one seemed to notice Bubba off in the corner, smiling vacantly as he rubbed the bruises from his tumble down the side of the rocky mesa. Had they looked closely, they would have seen, over and over, his lips forming the silent words, *Château Bubba, Château Bubba, Château Bubba.*

That would have looked nice on a bottle.

SATURDAY'S JOURNAL

JUST A WHIFF OF CEDAR GAP

ell, it's a drippy Saturday in Cedar Gap. The few sputters of rain that forced a bunch of people off the streets and into the Palace Cafe also gave them that brotherhood feeling of being the lone survivors of a temporary catastrophe.

Just a minute ago, Buddy Olitson, our token Yankee yuppie, walked in, took a deep sniff, and whispered, "All right!"

"Whatcha smell, Buddy?" Yancy McWhirter, our mayor, asked loudly. "Brenda Beth's stew?"

Buddy smiled broadly. "Nope. I smell Cedar Gap."

Some throats cleared as the room got very quiet. "Hey, wait a minute, guys, don't take it wrong. Get a noseful. Whaddaya smell?" A few tentative sniffs produced only quizzical looks. "Wet denim. Strong coffee. Straw. That's the smell of Cedar Gap, and I love it!" A few heads nodded slowly. A couple of nervous smiles. "You guys think I moved here from Pittsburgh just for the barbecue?"

The cafe relaxed into chuckles. "Aw, Buddy," Wilson Kruddmeier said, "If ya grow up with those smells, ya don't really notice 'em."

Buddy waved his arm in a circle. "Come here. Walk outside and smell the rain as it hits that hot pavement. You get sight, sound, and smell."

"Actually," Murph Gumpton muttered, "rain on hot dust is even better'n rain on hot concrete."

"You can go with your rain," Milo Shively said, "but the best smell in the world, I'm talkin' *anywhere*, is new-turned bottom land. Boy, I wish I could bottle that smell."

Yancy reached for the coffeepot. "Do you remember how it is, up about late October or early November, you walk out on your porch, take a deep breath an' smile because your neighbor just started the first wood fire of the season? And you can tell exactly whether he's burnin' mesquite or oak."

"Oh, yeah, those are good," Sybil Jorgenson said with a sigh, "but I'll swap you straight across three years of wood fires for one set of clean sheets flap-dried in a July sun. You can just flat smell that Texas sunlight on wind-dried sheets."

At that, little knots of conversation formed, with smells and memories of smells the central topic.

"You know how you get out your garden tiller about March, an' you open up the gas an' oil an' pour it in? Those two smells just naturally say, 'Come on, boy, let's turn some dirt!' "

"Well, gas 'n oil's good, but when I run my mower for the first time in the spring, an' then sit on the porch all sweaty with a quart Mason jar of mint ice tea an' smell those mowed weeds, I tell ya, heaven cain't be better'n that."

"Yesterday I sawed some lumber for a brooder house, an' that pine sawdust smelled sweet as honey."

"I stumbled onto my grandmother's scrapbook the other day. I wonder if that's what the Depression really smelled like?"

"You been back to the elementary school recently? You know somethin', they still use the exact same floor polish as when I was a kid! I smelled that the other day, and all I could think of was that I didn't have my math homework ready to hand in."

"Well, smell a banana, and tell me that ain't recess!"

Suddenly, Bubba Batey's excited voice cut through the cafe. "My uncle Mort's got a ol' stable where I played when I was a little bitty kid. When I walk back in that barn now, I smell old hay an' liniment an' harness an' horse-dookey, an' it's all I can do not to cry." Then, embarrassed at the sudden quiet, Bubba looked down at his coffee. "Course, mostly I don't."

Vera Frudenburg sighed deeply. "I just smelled rain on some-body's wool coat, and then I remembered I smelled that when my daddy carried me when the water was too deep."

All heads nodded. Brenda Beth stood with a faraway glaze on her eyes, the pot of new coffee cooling in her hand. "It wasn't just the smell of apple cobbler; it was who was making it." She shook her head. "Mama always smelled like biscuit flour."

I guess it was the wet wool and the biscuits that did it. The con-versations dribbled down and then quit. The women smiled at the memories, but the men suddenly stared real hard at their coffee cups. Of course, there wasn't much point in looking around right about then because all of the menfolk's eyes got blurred at the same time.

Pollen count must be high.

CHAPTER 5

ALL THE YOUNG-UNS'

LEARNIN' ISN'T IN SCHOOL

*he New Jukebox*

As we prove almost daily in Cedar Gap, there's a world of fine information out there free for the taking. All the perceptive watcher has to know is the difference between spectacular accident and life-changing knowledge.

Take our new Palace Cafe jukebox as a case in point.

Four months ago, Brenda Beth Kollwood, the owner-manager and main waitress of the Palace Hotel and Cafe, ran a low wall around a little-used corner of the cafe and hung a sign proclaiming that area the Palace Mafia Headquarters. It was for the sole use of our Cedar Gap teenagers. Some people thought of it as merely a way to get kids off the street and away from the big people eating barbecue or drinking coffee.

Then two boys propped up their suitcase-sized twin-speaker boom boxes for a duel to the death or deafness, whichever came first.

"All right," Brenda Beth said. "You want some noise. I'll tell you what I'll do. You raise five hundred dollars, and I'll supply the rest for a used jukebox." Her eyelids dropped. "But I set the song policies."

The kids washed cars, sold light bulbs, and painted fences. They sponsored the first cakewalk in forty-three years. Terrifying rides on a cable slide rigged from the top of the mesa got fifty cents a scream. If it would net a buck, they did it.

Ten days ago, the high schoolers flapped the last twelve dollars on Brenda Beth's counter. "Good job. Now, here's the rules."

She explained that since you can't pen up the sound, some high-quality accommodating was called for. "There's sixty slots on that machine. I get the first slot, but after that, every decade from the forties gets ten songs, except y'all get twenty. Here's five sheets of paper for committee sign-ups. You got exactly forty-eight hours, or I'll choose 'em all myself." The kids blanched at the thought. "It's the American way," Brenda Beth said. She turned to the rest of the cafe regulars. "Now, this also includes all you turkeys over voting age. Get a decade, or do without."

Wide grins washed across every face, saying, "Where's the problem? The ten greatest songs of all time came from my own teenage years."

This immodest euphoria lasted about seventeen seconds into each committee meeting.

"We cain't use your list. There's nothin' there but a buncha ol' Buddy Holly songs."

"Well, he was a Texas boy, so naturally we gotta . . ."

The World War II vets wanted ten variations on "Praise the Lord and Pass the Ammunition," but the women demanded "I Left My Heart at the Stage Door Canteen" and similar saccharine goo.

Bizarre names drifted out of the high school meeting. "If I don't get 'Hey, Tiger' by Toad Liver and the Pond Scum," an animated little blonde pleaded, "I'll just die. I mean I'll just *actually* die!"

"Aw, that song's all eaten up with girl germs. What we gotta do is get us five trucker songs an' five cheatin' songs an' five Texas songs an'—

"Watch it, pimple-monger!" a girl snarled. "You try ramroddin' that macho garbage around here, and you'll walk into school with a frown and a real funny limp."

One ol' boy, blinded by nostalgia and a slippery memory, said he wanted "anything by the Ezzard Charles Singers."

Finally it got down to the *real* American way: "Awright, I'll vote for your Madonna if you'll vote for my Springsteen."

Wednesday, Brenda Beth moved the scarred but serviceable used Rockola jukebox into Mafia Headquarters. With a flourish, she threw the switch.

Bulging red plastic glowed. Thin curved orange tubing bubbled. Blue lights flickered. And best of all, a quarter got the first selection, Bob Wills's "San Antonio Rose." Even the kids smiled at the justice of that selection.

Just now, Brenda Beth squinted against the rattling noise of a Hank Williams, Jr. epic of rejection and thirst. "I guess it was worth it, but I'll sure be glad when the novelty wears off and warm weather gets here."

"What'll you do till then?"

Brenda Beth grimaced. "Gimme a quarter." She sidled quietly up to the jukebox and punched a number just as Hank, Jr.'s nasal request for understanding and another long neck drifted to a close. A record lifted and twisted into place. But no sound came out.

"Somethin's wrong with your machine, B. B."

"Nope," she sighed. "It's workin' perfectly."

"But I cain't hear nothin'."

Brenda Beth squinted and nodded. "I figured this would happen, so I got a friend of mine in Fort Worth to make me a special five-minute record of dead air." She took a slow, deep breath. "Y'all are welcome to punch ol' Number One anytime the pain gets too great."

Just then, Toad Liver and the Pond Scum screeched something resembling "AAAAAA bleeet graaaaaap flaaaaaarmmmmm, Bay-BEEEEEE!"

Fourteen hands scratched frantically through pockets and purses for quarters.

The voting and the education, American-style, were off and running.

Braggin' Rights

There are those isolated times when, for unexplained reasons, the jukebox goes silent in the Palace Mafia Headquarters. That's usually the signal for any adults to listen up to the beginning of the newest edition of The World's Largest Exhibition of Reverse English.

It usually starts when somebody like T. J. Curnutt, Arnold and Dodie's youngest, walks in, slams a chair against the wall, and starts gritting his teeth.

"Hey, T. J.," a girl calls out, "you coming swimming this afternoon?"

T. J.'s eyes squint into little slits. "Naw. I gotta WORK all day."

"Work Monday. Saturday's for playing."

"Not if my pickup won't run. My pa said he bought me that ol' '68 Dodge, an' if I want wheels of any kind, it's my job to keep it runnin'." T. J. folds his arms dramatically. "I gotta tear down the differential, an' that's a full weekend outta my life."

"You can do that?" the girl says admiringly.

"Well," T. J. says, pride shoving aside his irritation, "Pa supervises some, but I do all the actual raw grunt-work." He glances sideways. The girl sits with her head cocked over, listening. "Pa makes me fix ever'thing on that truck."

Usually there's another boy, short and red-haired, gulping his Mountain Dew. "Huh, that's nothin'. My daddy got me three heifers and a little bull, and said, 'Boy, that's your college education. The better those animals live in that pasture, the better you'll live in college.'" The kid crushes the can. "I mean, I'll be takin' care of those fool animals for my whole academic career. And my ol' man's even makin' me shovel out our neighbor's barn to pay for the vaccinations." The boy pushes back his cowboy hat. "Dang, my daddy's tough on me."

"Shoot," a girl snorts. "At least you guys get to go outside and see sunshine once in a while. My last report card had two or three little ol' C's on it—I mean, not much of a problem at all—but I thought we were gonna have to sedate my mama when she saw it. She said I can't go anywhere outside the city limits until my grades average a B. I'll be forty-five and dead by that time!" She turns to a friend. "Aren't there some laws somewhere about child abuse?"

Another girl slurps her soda noisily. "Let me tell you about *real* child abuse. You'd think my folks were religious fanatics or Moonies or something the way they make us kids go to church. We're talking three times a week!"

"I've had it with my family. All I hear is 'Sit up straight!' Say 'yessir' an' 'nawsir' to anybody older'n me! Gag me with a tire iron."

"You know what my grandma did Tuesday night? Dragged me away from my favorite 'MASH' rerun that I've only seen six or seven times an' made me watch a sunset, I'm talkin' a SUNSET while she read a poem! I couldn't believe it!"

"How was the sunset?"

"Aw, you know, it was right after that rain, so it was . . . but I think she's losing it. She said that sunset was better'n 'MASH.' Now, come on, is my family the worst, or what?"

"Hey," a girl's voice pipes, "you guys remember that party we had a month ago? I HAD to have a new dress, right? My m-o-t-h-e-r dug out some fabric she was saving for something, pointed to the sewing machine, and said, 'The sooner you learn to sew, the sooner you're in style.' Now, I ask you, is that a mother's love?"

That's the way it goes for an hour, as every kid tops the last one with a tale of family sadism and heartlessness.

Finally, the kids drift away. The cafe gentles into a thoughtful stillness.

"I've heard braggin' in my time," Newton Jimson will say quietly, "but that buncha kids just beats ever'thin'."

"Now, Newt," Dolly Hooter says, "how else can they show the world the superiority of their own particular families than by giving examples of how mean their folks are to them?"

Waldo Beeler pours coffee all around. "That's all well an' good, but I know for a fact we didn't talk about our folks like that when we were kids."

"No, we didn't, Waldo," Oliver Greenslope agrees. "An' my ol' daddy wasn't as kind as these kids' parents, neither. I mean, he ruled! I either plowed five acres with that mule, or I didn't get supper."

"Huh! My daddy made me break the mule for ridin' first, *then* plow the five acres. He was some kinda pistol, my ol' daddy."

It always goes downhill from there. Grownups bragging about *their* parents can flat get sickening. You really don't want to hear about it.

Wildflowers for Katy

There are times when schooling gets its best results from external sources. Like the other day, when Wilson Kruddmeier's daughter Missy finished her research paper. I don't care how many infinitives she split or participles she hung out to dry, I know that paper is a keeper.

Missy's a bouncy, auburn-haired high school junior with a painful attitude problem. But a few days ago she walked slowly into the Palace Cafe, pushed a chair toward the cluttered plate glass window, and just sat there, staring and twisting a thread on her letter-jacket. It was obvious she was stifling a good cry.

Finally she sucked in a trembling breath. "You been to the cemetery?" I nodded. "All the way back to the old headstones?" I nodded again. A tear pulled a shiny track down one young, smooth cheek. "Miss Stilwell knew this would happen, didn't she?"

I shrugged. Lucille Stilwell, Missy's English teacher, knows that some seeds sprout, some don't. And attitude changes are always iffy.

Missy's been pressuring her parents constantly one way or another for a year or more. Then Lucille assigned Missy the topic "My People on the Back Lot."

Our Cedar Gap Cemetery is divided into two sections, the new lot up front and the older lot back a ways with gravestones dating before the turn of the century. Missy's assignment entailed telling a story from whatever information she could pick up from the carved headstones.

"Do you know those cheap headstones on the O'Reardon graves?" Missy wasn't looking at me, so I kept quiet. "They said they lost three-year-old twin girls and a newborn son in 1899, so I put that in my first draft. Miss Stilwell told me to rewrite it from the viewpoint of the father. I found some records in the court house that said Donald O'Reardon and his wife, Katy, came here from Ireland in 1892 so Donald could work on the railroad. Then Miss Stilwell asked how Katy O'Reardon felt about leaving Ireland."

Lucille Stilwell's motto is engraved above her chalkboard: "You don't write term papers; you *re*write term papers."

Missy leaned against the wall as she gazed at the quiet street. Her trembling lips muffled her words.

"Katy came to America when she was seventeen, the same age I am right now. When she was twenty-two, the twins and the new-born died in some kinda epidemic." Missy's shoulders sagged. "Katy buried them on a dry, brown, windblown West Texas hillside in January."

"Not many wildflowers out that time of year," I said.

Missy's dark curls bounced as she jumped at the sound of my voice. "I suppose not. When I handed Miss Stilwell my paper, she just said one thing: 'Tell me about the Irish.'"

Missy dabbed at the tears welling up in earnest. "Do you know how much people hated the Irish back then? I mean, they wouldn't even talk to them. Some preachers wouldn't bury their dead people, and the railroad Irish were treated worse than trash. That's when Miss Stilwell told me I was ready for a final draft about Katy and Donald's deaths."

I'd seen this coming. Lucille Stilwell's English composition classes have been changing kids for two decades and more. She keeps them digging until they get past the subject and down into themselves.

Missy talked for thirty minutes about Katy's grinding loneliness. Donald O'Reardon died less than two years after the twins and the newborn, probably in an accident while laying track or building a bridge over some nameless creek. Katy, alone and friendless, lasted only a year.

"She'd buried her babies. Her husband was in a cheap grave Katy may have dug herself. She was alone in a strange land, no money, and everyone hated her because she wasn't from around here. I don't know how she stayed alive. Maybe she worked in the railroad cookshed, or took in washing, or . . . whatever." Missy wiped her eyes. "All she wanted was a husband and her babies . . . and maybe one friend to talk to. She didn't want much." Missy riffled through some typed pages. "I guess compared to me, she didn't want anything. They buried her next to the twins with her name and dates scratched on a broken piece of stone somebody found out in the field." Missy waited a long time. "There wasn't anybody to tend her grave. There wasn't anybody to cry for her."

Just now, I walked over to the burying place and back to the old gravestones. Some little wildflowers leaned against Katy's rocky, untended grave. A few tiny wet spots glistened on the gravestone.

Katy finally found her friend.

The Motivating of No-Neck

Texas has traditionally placed a premium on individual effort, from Davy Crockett at the Alamo to how far somebody had to run to stomp out a brushfire. Also, being Texas, there is generally a permanent floating argument careening around the Palace Cafe about the greatest individual effort by a local athlete. By general consensus, No-Neck Noonan's charge onto the playing field is the prizewinner.

Elmore Noonan stands six feet six inches and weighs about two-fifty, but he looks bigger. True, his body has the bulk of your average mountain gorilla, but from his shoulders up it's a pure triangle. Hence the name No-Neck Noonan.

Two years ago, Corley Freemont, the coach of everything played with a ball at South Taylor County Junior College, took one look at No-Neck during freshman orientation and lost his mind. Avarice and greed poured out of Corley's eyes until he found out Elmore No-Neck Noonan was an English major who preferred playing in the band. It's not a pleasant thing to watch a coach both drool and cry when the band marches at halftime.

It's not that Elmore is against athletics, it's just that playing cymbals is, as he said, "soothing." The fact that he casts a shadow like a diesel earthmover doesn't mean he has to work like one. "Anyway," he explained, "I tried football in junior high, and it made me tired."

Corley Freemont tried appealing to No-Neck's patriotism, he tried insulting No-Neck's manhood, he even tried bribery, assuring No-Neck he could get him a pickup truck from the motor pool "anytime you wanna, you know, take a girl out sommeres." But No-Neck just shrugged off the blandishments, insisting that the Marching Gila Monster Band needed him and his flashing cymbals as geographic markers for their half-time shows.

For fifteen full seasons, the patient fans in Cedar Gap have cheered the Fighting Gila Monster football team's struggle toward the glory of a .500 season, only to suffer through a total collapse in the final games. But this season the stars and planets were in the right conjunction. The team entered the final game with a 7–2 record. The only thing standing between them and the conference title was the Hereford Junior College Bulls.

The score wobbled back and forth, with first one team, then the other giving away touchdowns until the final two minutes of the game when our Fighting Gila Monsters missed an extra point, leaving them on the crying end of a 40–39 score.

Suddenly, No-Neck Noonan began pacing the sidelines, cymbals held high. In his gray and green uniform he resembled a bloated swamp creature, and the cymbals, flashing in the setting sun like a tyrannosaurus rex with pinkeye, completed the primordial picture. No-Neck made no sound, only a lunging cornered-animal sort of motion toward the opposing team. All eyes, particularly those of the opposing quarterback, were on No-Neck's Cro-Magnon dance.

On the kickoff, the Hereford Bulls managed to stumble into a first down. With time running out, No-Neck bobbed back and forth and began babbling a drumlike chant. Suddenly, with ten seconds to go, No-Neck screamed like a panther, bowed his back—and split his uniform from knee to collar.

With a frantic lunge, he tore off the band coat, ripped a set of shoulder pads from a scrawny sub, and ran screeching and crow-hopping onto the dusty field.

Corley Freemont isn't the brightest light in the sky, but he knows a gift from heaven when he sees it. "Time! Noonan in for, Noonan in for . . . Cantrell, throw somebody off the field, and Noonan's in for him."

No-Neck wore his white marching spats without shoes, his gaping split britches, no shirt, and shoulder pads on backwards, which forced his head up and back, so that the Hereford Bulls' offensive line could stare directly up No-Neck's flaring nostrils. His bare chest resembled an oak keg with Brillo pads glued indiscriminately around it.

"Play the game!" the referee yelled and blew his whistle. The Hereford quarterback, abruptly realizing he would be the first man in forty thousand years to be eaten by a dinosaur, took the snap and backpedaled frantically.

No-Neck leaped straight into the air and screamed. By the time he hit the ground, the entire Hereford line had finished a group prayer of exorcism. The rest of the Fighting Gila Monsters just tippy-toed through the glazed-eyed Bulls, waited until the petrified quarterback staggered back across his own goal line, and then tackled him for a safety, two points, and the win as the final gun fired.

No-Neck turned majestically, grabbed the split seat of his pants with one hand, and walked serenely back to his beloved cymbals. He never played another down for the Fighting Gila Monsters.

He didn't need to. He was already a legend.

SATURDAY'S JOURNAL

THE BEST AND FINAL GIFT

ell, here it's the Saturday after Christmas in Cedar Gap, and some of the gifts have come in different wrappings.

Naomi Ruth Dickertson is a fiftyish widow eking out a living peddling cosmetics to lady Gapians to support her daughter April and her confused mother, Fannie Lusker. Grandma Fannie got along fairly well until about five years ago when her memory quirks expanded and joined. Now she just stares out the window, rocking and occasionally mumbling incoherently.

When school let out a week ago, April found herself with that frightening commodity, preadolescent spare time. "Mom, can I go on your route with you?" No. "Can we go shopping when you're done?" No. "Well, I'm bored."

Naomi Ruth snapped, "Boredom's your problem, money's mine. Go talk to your grandmother."

April's face twisted into a fist. "She doesn't know anything. Grandma just sits there and stares. She won't even talk anymore." But desperate boredom finally drove April to her vacant-eyed, silent grandmother.

"Grandma Fannie," April whispered, "you awake?" The old woman slowly turned her blank gaze from the window. "Grandma Fannie, I think I'm going to go crazy, I'm so bored."

Fannie tilted her wrinkled face and frowned.

"Were you ever bored when you were my age?" April asked.

The bent gray woman sucked in a slow, trembling breath. It was just the jumpstart her rusty mind needed. "Let's see, now, you're . . ."

"April," the girl said, startled at the strength of her grandmother's words.

"And how old are you, April?"

"I'm twelve."

"April's twelve." Slowly, laboriously, old musty tunnels of Fannie Lusker's mind began opening. "I was twelve . . . when the Big War started."

"What war, Grandma?"

"The Kaiser's war."

"What's a Kaiser?"

"A Kaiser . . . a Kaiser . . ." Fanny hesistated. "We called him Kaiser Bill, and he wore a . . . wore a . . ." Her finger scratched at her lip.

"A . . . mustache?

"Big thick rascal of a . . . mustache." Fannie's mouth curled into a slow smile. "And a tin hat with a little pointy arrow on top." She exhaled several times in an approximation of a laugh.

April bent closer. "Did you ever see this Kaiser Bill?"

"Oh, child, he lived in . . . in . . . Germany!" Her gray eyebrows shot up. "I haven't thought about him in . . ."

"Grandma Fannie, you never told me that story. How old were you then?"

"I'm fifteen." Fannie's eyes glistened. "It's my fifteenth birthday."

April sat back, confused. "This is your birthday?"

"Oh yes, and thank you for remembering." Like water when a plug has been kicked out of a rain barrel, Fannie's stream of words tumbled out clear and pure. Her crackling voice wheezed out the old songs "Over There" and "K-K-K-Katy." Wrinkled fingers pointed to imaginary bows and lace on a party dress she made for herself.

For an hour, April asked questions and listened with troubled fascination as her grandmother raced through descriptions of Cedar Gap boys who died in the War to End All Wars and of the girls who waited. Suddenly her grandmother leaned forward, her face animated, her voice a birdlike song. "And now . . . Elton's come home." Her crooked parchment-like hands clapped with joy. "And we're getting married!" Fannie's old eyes focused on the horizon as she strained for more words. "We're getting . . . married . . . and then . . . and this house . . . and we'll be so happy . . ."

The old woman eased back against the rocker and closed her eyes. The spring had run dry. Her lips fumbled at a few words, but finally, with a sigh, they quieted into a smile. Her eyes slowly closed.

April tiptoed out. When Naomi Ruth finished her Christmas route around Cedar Gap, April hit her at the door with all of the stories from Grandma Fannie.

Naomi Ruth frowned in disbelief. "Mama said those things? I'd better look in on her." Two minutes later, Naomi Ruth walked slowly into the kitchen. Her eyes blinked back tears. "April," she said carefully, "get Doc Winslow." When April started to protest, Naomi Ruth said quietly, "Mama's dead." She wiped at her eyes, then whispered, "You should see her smile! Like she'd just been given a wonderful gift."

April walked out the door, frowning. At twelve, death held more fascination than fright, but she was curious. "A gift?" she thought. "I didn't give her any gift. I just talked to her and she talked to me. What kind of a gift is that?"

For a final gift, the best.

CHAPTER 6

CARS 'N PICKUPS 'N OTHER

USEFUL ART OBJECTS

urt's Car at the Gas-N-Git

Today is exactly four days after the night Newton Jimson fixed Burt Reynolds's Jaguar out at Newton's Gas-N-Git on the highway. It sure does seem longer than just four days.

You've got to understand that up until sundown four days ago, the biggest thing in Newt Jimson's life was World War II and the twenty-seven hours he spent on a troopship anchored at Honolulu. As Newt puts it almost daily, "Those were the most critical hours of the whole war. Our unit had been carefully trained to invade Japan, an' without doubt, they'd heard of us. Oh, yeah, they'd heard of us!" Newt was a clerk for the motor pool.

But back to four days ago. As Newt tells it, just as Johnny came on the television, this shiny gray car shaped like a banana with a goiter wheezed under the canopy of his gas station-convenience store and stopped. A guy he thought he knew unloaded out of the tiny door of the long sports car and frowned. Luther Gravely, our area inebriate, roused himself long enough to nod and say, "Howdy, Burt," then collapsed back in his wicker chair.

Newt failed in his attempt to look casual as he broke the story early Wednesday morning at the Palace. "Burt was tired from a long day of shooting an' a wrap party over around Seminole, an' he was trying to make it to San Antonio to catch the red-eye back to L.A."

Newt's watched the "Tonight Show" since Jack Paar had it, so he probably thinks he knows what he's talking about. At any rate, Burt's rented Jaguar was obviously suffering from some undefined, possibly terminal, affliction.

"Whadja do, Newt?" somebody asked.

"Well, I asked Burt what was wrong, an' he said the engine was about to quit, an' asked if I could fix it. I told him about my experience with our motor pool back at Fort Hood, an' he smiled real big. I could see he was impressed." Newt took a slow sip of coffee.

"What'd he look like, Newt?"

"Aw, you know Burt, he ain't changed. Course, I hadn't seen him for close on to ten years, but he still looks good."

"Hey, come on, Newt! When'd you see Burt Reynolds live?"

Newt straightened and frowned. "Listen, I saw him in Houston at that Oilers-Cowboys game, an' I was as close to him as from me to you. He looks just like he did then."

"Whadja do then, Newt?"

What Newt actually did wasn't important; it was only important how Newt described it. Lifting the lid of that Jaguar took on the dimensions of opening King Tut's tomb. "I had him fire up the engine, an' real quick I saw some smoke comin' outta the side a the engine. I asked him if he had a little tool kit that came with the car—those Limey cars are real persnickety an' need special tools—an' he got out this package that must have been real leather, 'cause it . . ."

"Whadja do then, Newt?"

"I'm gettin' to it! There was a little tool bent like an S, an' I just twisted that in a bracket holdin' the smog pump an' the smoke stopped an' the engine took off, smooth as corn silk. Boy, Burt was happy! He tried to pay me, but I told him what's a friend for. He told me if I uz ever in Hollywood, to look him up an' he'd buy me lunch. Burt's just that kinda guy. Always has been."

Wednesday afternoon, the story sparkled with more conversational gambits and examples of his and Burt's wit and comradery, like swapping jokes and how Burt appreciated Newton's thoughts on his latest films.

Thursday, we learned that Burt originally heard about Newton's repairing genius clear up around Snyder and had just limped along until he could get to the Gas-N-Git and Newton's fabled expertise.

Friday, the story took on Homeric dimensions when Newton let it slip that Burt had asked Newton for advice on his love life.

Then today, the worst thing possible happened. A thin package came to the post office. Bertie Faye Hogg, the postmistress, took one look at the return address and ran the package over to Newton who was coffeeing up with the rest of the crowd at the Palace Cafe. Inside was an eight-by-ten glossy photograph reading, "To Newton, a friend and automotive genius of the finest kind, with sincere gratitude." It was signed "Burt Reynolds."

Cedar Gap was doomed.

Ferrell's New Car

Ugly as it is, Ferrell's One-One-Twelve has been accepted by a fairly critical public. He bought his current means of transportation when his other new car lost a duel with a semi.

Ferrell Epperson is the supervisor of the highway department district office, and he's always driven a Dodge or Ford or something domestic. But this new car was assembled about ten thousand miles west of Tacoma, which irritates and confuses the local citizenry. It was a good enough car, if you like skateboards.

"Hey, Ferrell," Travis Breedlow yelled, "I think ya lost the blade off your ridin' mower." There was a lot of that sort of thing.

The problem wasn't so much that it was a foreign car as the fact that it wasn't a pickup. Around Cedar Gap, you go to work or to town in a pickup truck, and you go to Grandma Minnie's on Sunday in a car. Waldo Beeler stocks a few used cars at his lot, Beeler's Fine Used Trucks and Tractors, but they're slow movers.

"I never seen anything like it. I cain't sell car one, unless it's twenty years old."

"Why so old, Waldo?"

"'Cause back then, you could fix your own. Now, ever'thin's electric—the transmission, the fuel pump, even the doorlocks. I got a '85 on my lot with the battery down an' the doors locked, an' I cain't even get into it."

"Is that the blue one looks like a lima bean?"

"Yeah, or a declawed armadillo. Did somebody pass a law against puttin' corners on a car?"

Ferrell bought his little Oriental zipper because he heard they got about a thousand miles to the gallon. "The man up in Abilene promised me faithful I could drive round-trip to Houston for a dollar six bits."

Ferrell just about got to the point of some gentle bragging about the car—"Listen, I can turn around in my garage with the overhead door down"—and could almost ignore the joshing insults—"Ya know, Ferrell, that'd make a tolerable fine anchor for a trotline"—when the disaster struck.

Bubba Batey, our low-wattage roadside grass mower, was trimming up part of the roadside park a mile north of here with a frontloader when Ferrell dropped by to check out Bubba's work. Just as Ferrell parked his tiny car, a huge Peterbilt reefer swung wide to avoid a deer and lost control.

The semi scrunched Ferrell's car against a huge boulder, warping its frame and jamming all doors and windows. It also ruptured the gas line under the hood. Flames shot out over the bumper and the front wheels.

"It was well nigh the worst three minutes of my life. I yelled at Bubba to stay away 'cause the gas tank might blow any minute."

Instead, Bubba ignored the potential for fire or explosion as he scooped up the crumpled car in the bucket of his front-loader. He bounced across a bar ditch, annihilated two fences, then dropped the dripping car unceremoniously in a wide place in Sybil Jorgenson's creek.

"I don't know which was worse, watching Dolly Hooter bouncing around with her little Instamatic trying to get my exclusive picture for the *Galaxy-Telegraph* or having to live with the idea that my tombstone's gonna read *Bubba Batey Saved His Life*."

Now Ferrell's back driving sort of an improvised domestic flatbed that Ambrosio Gonzales, the intuitive mechanic-owner of the Old Chihuahua Auto Repair, cobbled out of a wrecked '47 Chevy dump-truck cab, a John Deere motor, and some oak packing crates.

"It's not much for pretty," Ferrell said proudly, "but it's heck for stout." He patted the rough oak planking. "And it'll start no matter how cold or hot the day. I call it my One-One-Twelve."

Since we assumed the oddity was strictly one of a kind, somebody asked if that was its model number.

"Nope. It means that one gallon of gas and one quart of oil will get me twelve miles." He frowned. "But I'm having trouble register-ing it."

"Cain't find the serial number?"

"Worse than that. The lady at the courthouse says she can only register things that began life as some kind of a recognizable vehicle."

All the heads nodded. For sure, that would rule out Ol' One-One-Twelve.

Ambrosio's Apprentice

Truble's gone, but his memory lingers on. Ambrosio's seeing to that.

About six months ago, our South Taylor County Junior College, in its striving for relevancy, started a free-form class called *General Repairing 101* where the students hire out to local craftsmen for the final hands-on polishing of their book learning.

Gunther Burns, our area drapery expert, snorted. "Teach some-body to cut straight on a bias, and you got somebody I can hire."

Corley Freemont, the coach of everything at STCJC, poured some more coffee. "I dunno. Service an' repair are the trouble-spots in our economy. If you can fix somethin', you'll have a job."

Ambrosio Gonzales listened quietly to the Palace Cafe chatter. Ambrosio's intuitive approach to equipment resuscitation has kept vehicles and appliances operative when other fixers give up in dis-gust. That afternoon, Ambrosio visited STCJC.

"I'm sorry, Mr. Gonzales," the director of the program said, "but all our students have been placed."

Ambrosio nodded at a thin blond boy bent under the hood of a surplus army Jeep. "Whare eez theez wan working?"

The director frowned into the gloom of the auto shop. "Aw, Truble don't really count. I'm just lettin' him use some tools to fix a busted tie-rod." The man shrugged and whispered. "I had some problems with Truble. He didn't wanta fix things the way the manual says to."

Ambrosio smiled and nodded. "How do I sign heem op?"

Truble Blander's frowning belligerence masked a debilitating lack of self-confidence. Slowly, quietly, Ambrosio showed him how to substitute for a shock absorber when none was available. He learned to improvise a radiator, fix an obsolete brake drum, and weld a homemade windscreen on a tractor. Ambrosio even showed Truble how to make his own tools when none would fit. Truble spent his extra time sorting through a pile of spare parts from vehicles dating back to a World War I motorcycle and a '24 Essex.

Then Ambrosio startled the withdrawn, sullen boy. "Tomorrow, make sawmtheeng that works." Truble's eyes lit up.

Throughout the night, Truble pawed through warped wheels, broken springs, and misshapen sheet iron. The blue flicker of a welding torch greeted early risers. At midmorning, he ripped the leather off the seats of a discarded bus. By noon, he was bolting and welding again. At four o'clock, Truble shoved something vaguely resembling a two-place hammock-on-wheels out of Ambrosio's shop.

Ambrosio nodded slowly. "What does eet do?"

"It's a two-man planter for gettin' tomato plants or somethin' else in the ground." Truble flopped face-down into one of the leather hammock-like holders. "One guy drives the tractor, two guys lay belly-down and plant. I heard about one once."

Ambrosio picked up his phone and called a farmer in Merkel. Within the hour, the man stood staring at the homemade contraption. "Make that so it'll hold four people, an' I'll give you one thousand dollars for it." Ambrosio whistled. The man shrugged. "Listen, anything like that from a commercial firm would cost five thousand dollars. You want a job at my place fixing my machinery?"

Truble frowned at the attention and the money. He glanced at

Ambrosio. "Naw, maybe later. Right now I'm still workin' for Mr. Gonzales."

Truble spent the night living on caffein and raw nerves as he revised a wrecked '86 Buick. By sunrise, he'd reworked the entire trunk assembly so it could be ratcheted up or down, or stay at any height.

Ambrosio nodded and smiled appreciatively. "Very nice." He turned. "Let's call General Motors."

Truble stepped back, shocked. "I didn't break no law doin' that, did I?"

"No, no! But eet ees too good an idea to keep in Cedar Gap. Here, you talk."

Truble talked. GM listened. Two executives arrived and bought the idea on the spot. One executive shook Truble's hand. "We got forty guys on full salary, and not a one of them thought to try it your way." He squinted at the machinery. "I don't suppose you have any more ideas, do you, Mr. Blander?"

Truble glanced at Ambrosio. "Maybe one or two. I'll give you a call." Ambrosio smiled proudly.

Yesterday, Truble moved an hour's drive, to Coleman, where he opened his own free-form repair shop. But he's not really gone. His picture hangs in the Old Chihuahua Repair Shop under a sign Ambrosio proudly welded from some oil-well sucker rods and a Dodge pickup tailgate. The sign reads: *Famous Great Mechanics of Cedar Gap*.

Who would know better?

SATURDAY'S JOURNAL

THE OLD AIRPORT

ell, here it is Saturday morning again in Cedar Gap, and the mayor is still looking for matching federal funds. Yancy Mc-Whirter patterns his mayoral career after the leaders of Dallas and Houston; that is, be photographed in a hard hat at construction sites and try to squinch up to the federal trough.

Basically, Mayor Yancy is like a coonhound pup: big feet, lots of noise, and fairly useless but fun to watch if he doesn't break anything valuable. But last weekend, he stalked into the Palace Hotel and Cafe for the biweekly town council breakfast and boldly stated, "We're fixin' up the old airport."

The problem with the old airport is just that: It's an ancient, weed-covered, semi-horizontal single runway a little longer than a football field but considerably narrower. Back in the early twenties, a piece of unused county property was leveled so barnstormers could take up Cedar Gapians for a dollar a head. About the time of the advent of Piper's original Cub, the town council tacked up what was to be the last major capital improvement on the airport, a wind sock. The airport didn't even have a name; it's always been just "the old airport."

Thus, when Yancy said, "We're fixin' up the old airport," the general reaction was lethargic disbelief. But the gleam in Yancy's eyes said, "I'm gonna earn that dollar a year you pay me."

Sunday afternoon, Bubba Batey borrowed the highway department's mower and scalped the worst of the thistles and volunteer side oats covering the runway area. A bunch of people walked out to laugh and then stayed to straighten fencepoles and tighten rusty barbed wire.

Monday, four of the women in the Cedar Gap Floral Artistry and Brunch Club straddled their riding mowers and discovered that all of that stubble hid a fairly nice turf. They even found the steel hoop from the old wind sock, which one of the clubbers refurbished in garish Day-Glo colors that could be seen in El Paso.

It became the thing to do of an evening to walk out to see the old airport. Yancy was usually there to explain its importance as a symbol of Cedar Gap's future, but Thursday, Yancy vanished and didn't reappear until Friday morning when he commandeered the microphone of KCDR-FM, our little 250-watt country-western station. He ordered everyone out to the airport at ten o'clock Saturday morning for one of the great events in Cedar Gap history. Even the *Cedar Gap Galaxy-Telegraph* stopped its giant press to insert a two-inch headline: SATURDAY—BE THERE.

Today was one of those perfect Texas mornings, almost no wind and a few puffy cotton-boll clouds in a cobalt sky. By nine-thirty, the whole town stood around oohing and aahing at the improvements. Old-timers recalled when they last saw a Jennie or a Stearman or a Tin Goose fly into the little grass strip.

At exactly ten o'clock, somebody yelled and pointed. A tiny sunflower-yellow plane that could only be Milo Shively's crop duster popped over our mesa and made three passes at about fifty feet, trailing red, white, and blue smoke. Then it stood on one wing, did a 360, and plopped onto the runway of the Cedar Gap Airport, the first plane to land there in four decades. Milo waved, then pulled forward his pilot's seat. Out hopped Yancy, grinning like a possum eating a green persimmon.

At a signal from Yancy, Ambrosio Gonzales drove his old '37 Diamond-T flatbed winch truck up to the airport gate. Swinging from the winch was a sign Ambrosio had welded from bits of copper gas line and the bumpers off an old Pierce-Arrow. The sign read *Veterans Memorial Airport, Cedar Gap, Texas*. Everyone applauded, and someone yelled, "Awright!"

Suddenly, far on the south horizon, four airplanes appeared in a diamond formation. They came on slow and low, then somebody yelled, "It's the Confederate Air Force from Harlingen." Two old Corsairs, a B-26, and a twin-boomed P-38 Lightning lumbered through their flyby.

Just as they passed directly overhead, the Lightning pulled right and up to disappear over our mesa in a "missing-man" formation honoring lost comrades.

There wasn't a sound—no wind, no coughing, only a little snuffling from two World War II VFW members.

Somebody started to sing "Oh, say can you see . . ." very softly. The song moved through the crowd like wind through a wheatfield.

It's been sung louder. It's been sung faster.

But it's never been sung better.

CHAPTER 7

SPEAKING BASIC PUDGINIAN

he Expert Expatriot

There are those who say that Cedar Gap is near kin to atomic fallout: the closer the proximity, the more you take on its characteristics.

Now, that may be just a bit too much. No one around here, to our knowledge (Luther Gravely notwithstanding), glows in the dark. On the other hand, there is a certain truth to the fact that once you're exposed to the Cedar Gap life-style and philosophy, it's tougher to shake than malaria. Moving away may alter a bit of the vocabulary, and you may not wear blue jeans to church as much, but the virus is still hunkered down, waiting for just the right moment to erupt.

Take Rudy Pudgins. He came to mind about a month ago when his bimonthly letter arrived.

Rudolph Pudgins grew up here in Cedar Gap, so he bills himself the Cedar Gap Expert Expatriot. As Luther, our area inebriate, explains it, "*Ex-pert* comes from two Latin words—*ex* meaning 'has-been,' and *spurt*, 'a drip under pressure.'" Which pretty well covers Rudolph Pudgins.

Five years ago, Rudy moved west after he got a two-word part in a movie shot down near San Angelo. He played a waiter asking Jimmy Stewart, "More tea?"

From that towering beginning, he moved to Hollywood, changed his name to Rock Pudgins, then to Blake Pudgins, then to J. R. Pudgins. Rudy retired from the movies to move to Tuba City, Arizona. His Korean War disability pension keeps him in beans and beer, and he cadges paper and pencils from the Motel 6 for our letters.

"Dear Gappies: Ptui," he starts. Rudy always spits after any derivation of his natal city's name.

"I hear your groveling, hog-slobber mayor is still sitting on his fatuous reputation instead of organizing the Cedar Gap (ptui) Fine Arts Concert Series, like I suggested last month. Have you any idea the benefits that accrue to a progressive metropolis with a wide-ranging arts base?"

Rudy played bass drum for one semester with the South Taylor County Junior College Marching Gila Monster Band right after high school, and his sensibilities for artistic endeavors have been in the ascendancy ever since.

"How can you hold your heads high knowing your people will never hear live the music of Bach and Bernstein? Imagine the coverage in the Dallas papers when the Berlin Philharmonic performs in Cedar Gap (ptui)."

Our only auditorium, the one at the elementary school, would just about hold the string section of the Berlin Philharmonic if the audience were willing to watch through the windows.

"I can hear you now, Mayor Yancy McWhirter, mewling that there's no place to perform. Predictably, you forgot the band shell in City Park. Well, expand that shell. Anticipate growth! *Plan for your children's children!!*"

Before he left, Rudy tried to appropriate land for an industrial park. Unfortunately, his appropriation included three square miles of Sybil Finkelbein Jorgenson's best stripper wells. When Sybil heard about it, she tried to run Rudy down with her '47 Studebaker, yelling that "We need an industrial park like Adam needed a belly button!"

"Dreams!" Rudy writes. "That's what you need in Cedar Gap. Ptui, and again I say Ptui!! Imagine (a word obviously beyond your driveling comprehension) the Chicago Symphony and Chorus opening with Mahler's 'Symphony of a Thousand,' continuing in December with the Tokyo String Quartet, followed in February with the Metropolitan Opera's touring production of *Aida*, and topped off in May by the two-hundred-member Edinburgh Military Tattoo."

As Rudy's letter was read, Dolly Hooter, staff reporter for the *Cedar Gap Galaxy-Telegraph*, stood up, mad as a cornered javelina. "Wait a minute! I've had it with that cowardly runaway. He completely overlooks the fact that Cody Cuttshaw and his Side B Band plays for our dance once a month, I mean *every* third Thursday, right upstairs in the ballroom of this Palace Hotel and Cafe."

"Right!" Gunther Burns said. "An' they must have, what, five people in the Side B Band alone, an' ever' one of 'em's got six strings on their guitars. What's this four-stringed Jap quartet nonsense? Cody beats 'em ever' day a the week, an' twice on Sundays."

"Hey, Rudy's been away a long time. He don't know that Saturday afternoons we can pick up rebroadcasts of 'A Prairie Home Companion.' I mean, what's Rudy want, anyway?"

"An' don't forget those halftime shows at the junior high over at Tuscola. Those thirty-two kids can flat march."

"Aw, well, Rudy's accelerator pedal always was stuck flat on the floorboard. Listen, I been to Edinburgh, an' it's just an average, middlin' South Texas town. I mean, who'd want to watch a buncha South Texas soldiers get tattooed? Rudy's just crazy."

At that point, Rudolph Pudgins's letter pretty well lost its focus. He asked if American Airlines had been contacted about moving its corporate headquarters to the Cedar Gap (ptui) Industrial Park or if Beeler's Fine Used Trucks and Tractors ever got that Maserati dealership.

It's just as well those questions never surfaced. The conversation was already flowing like a wet-weather culvert after a two-inch rain.

Rudy loves this town, he truly does. You've just got to know how to translate Pudginian. If you ever forget his Rushmorian compulsion to nudge this community along the pike toward major-city status, you could misconstrue his letters.

Rudy's Olympic Meet

For instance, his most recent letter took us to task for overlooking an obvious possibility for metropolitan immortality.

"Dear Gappies; Ptui!" You must never forget his salival punctuation. "You're too LATE *AGAIN*!! Seoul has come and gone, and somebody else already has the next Olympics. And I suppose, in true Gapian (ptui) fashion, you'll fizzle and flap around until it's too late to put Cedar Gap (paaaaahtui) on the list of possibilities for the next Olympics." Everything Rudy writes seems as if it would look better in italics. "Obviously, you've never considered the natural qualifications of West Texas!"

Dolly Hooter, ace stringer reporter for the *Cedar Gap Galaxy-Telegraph* and official reader of Pudginian communication, grimaced as she laid down the letter. "Rudy's right. In my entire life, I never once considered Cedar Gap as an international sports center."

"Hey, come on, Dolly," Waldo Beeler said, "maybe Rudy's hit somethin' for a change. We got a buncha things here that'd be perfect."

"Like what?"

"Well, for one thing, we could have a tractor pull. I mean, pull a *real* tractor. Let's get one a them Commies that's all pumped up with steroids and tie him to my ol' Farmall Cub. Let's see him pull *that* up the side a the mesa. We got some real men for that event right here in the area. I heard about a guy from down at Novice who single-handedly shoved his John Deere outta the way of a train."

Leonard Ply tilted his chair against the wall. "Actually, I know that ol' boy. He was workin' on his third six-pack, and he thought he saw a steam train on Highway 84 driven by a horned skeleton wearin' a red suit. When he tried to jump off his tractor, he hung his belt on the gear shift. He yanked that John Deere a quarter mile sideways."

"Well, there ya go!" somebody said. "We just gotta motivate our people for the right events. Like shinny."

"What's *shinny*?"

"It's a lot like hockey, but all it takes is a beat-up tin can, some knobby sticks, an' a rough ol' field with some oil drums for goals."

"Yeah! Let's get that sissy Russian hockey team an' challenge 'em to play shinny with some of our ol' boys late of a Saturday night. I'll guarantee we'll make a pianner keyboard outta leftover Russian teeth."

"Okay, while we're at it, let's give a prize for the highest flatfooted jump when scared by a rattler."

"Shoot, no contest there! I seen Bubba Batey go to the top of a twelve-foot load of oat-straw without even bendin' his knees. If screamin' don't count off, Bubba's got it."

"Yep, or how far you can throw a wrench when you've barked your knuckles on a stripped bolt."

"An' don't forget stompin' out grassfires. You 'member that time Wilson Kruddmeier's pickup backfired an' he set fire to his front forty? He stomped out three acres before the tanker truck got there. My mother-in-law'd make a great mixed-team entry all by herself."

Brenda Beth Kollwood set down a tray of coffee cups and a fresh pot. "I think the Olympic committee wants something with a bit more finesse."

"Finesse, huh?" Murphy Gumpton waved his hand. "Okay, let's let one of them Ay-rabs try filchin' an egg out from under a settin' banty hen. Naw, better than that, let 'em pick up a newborn calf an' then outrun the mama cow. Course, that'd turn it into a field event."

"Or ballet if they count off for steppin' in somethin'."

"Or we could have ever'body just keep eatin' Brenda Beth's four-alarm chili, an' the last one standin' wins."

"How about a tobacker spit? Four prizes: distance, volume, accuracy, an' tidy chins."

Dolly Hooter gazed solemnly at Rudy's letter, then thumbtacked it to the Palace Cafe's bulletin board. "I'll leave this up here in case anybody wants to call Washington and volunteer us." There were no takers.

Letting Rudy's ideas go public is a lot like shooting a bullet through a water tower—a lot of noise followed by an unstoppable and unusable flow.

But that's all right. Rudy believes in us. And we believe in Rudy. Ptui.

SATURDAY'S JOURNAL

ZACCHEUS AND OTHA:

HUMANITARIANS

ell, it's Saturday again in Cedar Gap, and Zaccheus and Otha Tatum are sleeping in.

Those two are special. They're black.

They're not special because they're black; they're special because they're Zach and Otha.

As the only black folks in Cedar Gap, they take their responsibilities seriously. They know that outside of the Cosbys and the NBA, they and their two kids are about the only nonwhites our elementary-school students will ever see. They tote that sizable burden proudly and well.

Zach, big and quiet, drives the lead mower for the highway department and farms his acre and a half on the east edge of town clear to the fenceposts. Little bitty Otha cans or freezes anything that won't flinch when you step on it. Their elderly house is surrounded by a couple of dozen fruit trees and a big old Spanish oak.

Which is where the trouble started.

Last Sunday morning Zaccheus showed up at the Cedar Gap Baptist Church all by himself, looking thin-lipped and tired. He slipped out during the invitation song without talking to anybody.

Sunday night, same thing, except Otha came alone.

"Zach 'n Otha haven't been to church by themselves since Moses came over on the ark," the Baptist pastor mumbled.

Monday, when Zaccheus bought a roll of chicken-wire, somebody said he looked like he'd been rode hard and put away wet.

Nobody saw them from Tuesday to Thursday. Then Friday morning, Bertie Faye Hogg, our postmistress, wandered into the Palace Cafe looking worried. "Zach hasn't picked up his mail for three days. Anybody heard from them?"

Ferrell Epperson, Zach's supervisor at the highway department, looked up. "Zach phoned in sick this whole week." He frowned at the sudden quiet. "Anybody for goin' down an' seein' about 'em?" Every hand went up.

The trip down Main Street resembled the torchlight parade in *Young Frankenstein*. People gathered like grit to a rolled snowball, finally stopping by the Tatums' green picket fence.

Otha, her thin frame haggard and wary, walked out on her front porch. She surveyed the group carefully. "Watchin' fifty white folks walk into a black man's front yard ain't designed to settle an upset stomach. Anything I can do for you?"

Several people mumbled the beginnings of sentences, but finally Ferrell blurted out, "Otha, we were worried about you two. Where's Zach?"

"Out back, with the babies."

Heads swiveled, eyes squinted, and mouths formed the silent word, "Babies?"

"Go see," she commanded.

Drunk soldiers creeping through a minefield would have looked more organized. Zaccheus looked up and frowned. "Didn't know we had us such a big ornothological club in town. You come to see the baby birds?"

"Naw," Ferrell said, "we come to see about . . . baby birds? I thought you were sick."

Zaccheus pointed up in the Spanish oak. "What I said was, we had a weakness at our house, and I had to see about it." He pointed up at the tree. "Those little things needed some protection, and they were on my land, so I stayed home."

"Those little things" was a nest of four tightly-packed baby scissor-tailed flycatchers. The mama bird hopped back and forth on the head-high limb, scolding the gawking crowd.

Zach stretched wearily. "Otha 'n me's been up night and day since Saturday keeping our old tomcat and two crib-robbing grackles from killing our baby birds."

"We been livin' on No-Doz," Otha said. "We had to . . . *Whoooop! Look out!*" Suddenly one of the tiny birds fluttered to the ground. The mother bird flopped down beside the pinfeathery baby, alternately pecking at it and covering it with her wings. Zaccheus leaped for his old cat and held it tightly while the mother bird completed her baby's preflight checkout.

Abruptly, the baby bird leaped and strained its wings until finally, to the accompaniment of fifty sucked-in breaths, the aerodynamically questionable baby bird skimmed up and over Zach's temporary chicken-wire fence to land in a mesquite thicket, squawking proudly. Twenty-five people applauded as the other twenty-five shushed them.

Ferrell gave Zach the rest of the day off for family recoverance.

"Besides," Ferrell said, "we can count it as a public-health act. Growed-up scissortails eat about five hundred flyin' bugs ever' day. We're lookin' at, what, a minimum of two thousand dead mosquitoes a day."

As I said, it's Saturday. The other three baby birds are flying. Zaccheus and Otha Tatum are sleeping in.

R. I. P.

CHAPTER 8

THE CHURCH OF THE

APOSTOLIC BELIEVERS

 *raven Image on South Street*

Without doubt, you've heard about the flap down at the Cedar Gap Independent Full Gospel Non-Denominational Four Square Missionarian Church of the Apostolic Believers. The leading edge of the hurricane moved in when Pastor T. Edsel Pedigrew, the spiritual leader of his flock of thirty-nine highly individualistic and vocal sheep, announced, "Our fine Church of the Apostolic Believers is commissioning an original artwork to inspire our members toward more Spirit-filled lives." That's Spirit with a Big *S*.

That came as a stark surprise. Being Fundamentalists—that's with a Big *F*—the Apostolic Believers take each microscopic phrase of Holy Writ for whatever can be wrung from it. No makeup, no jewelry, no shorts, no fun. And no graven images.

That's number two on the Big List of Commandments. Notice, those are not called the Ten Mild Suggestions. They are not considered as the Almost a Dozen Fairly Stout Ideas. When it says, "Thou shalt not take unto thee any graven images," then that's it, right there in the Received Original English, just like Charlton Heston wrote it.

"What kinda artwork we talkin' about, T. Edsel?"

"Big. Six feet tall, eight feet across, oil on plaster."

"Plaster? Why not canvas like Rembrandt an' Beethoven used?"

"'Cause the wall behind the baptistry is plaster."

For a century or more, every sure-nuff, thigh-high, water-up-the-nose Texas baptistry has featured some spiritual fresco designed to inspire and serious up all Watchers and Holy Ones. These scenes normally include a range of snow-capped alps, with golden aspens cascading down to a six-foot-wide Sea of Galilee. In other words, a typical West Texas vista.

"Who's doin' the paintin', T. Edsel?"

"We got us a spiritual man from up in Abilene." That's spiritual with a small *s* since none of the Abilene artists are Apostolic Believers. Actually, two of the potential painters are ABs, but one openly denies the divinity of the Four Square segment of the denomination, and the other is an Anti-Missionarian Apostolic Believer, which shoots him totally out of reach of either close fellowship or holy paint money.

The whole idea came originally from Delmarine Pedigrew, T. Edsel's lard-legged wife. Over an RC Cola and a Moon Pie, she decided the Apostolic Believers could accrue uncountable saintly benefits from visual as well as aural stimulation during their Sunday meetings.

And they could have—until the notion came up for discussion in the Adult Sunday School Class, where the impassioned arguments ricocheted from Socratic to Falwellian.

First, they'd always had cracked bare plaster above the lave of the baptismal pond, so historical justification for plainness was established.

Second, the Apostle Paul obviously detested baptismal art, a self-evident deduction since his unbounded hatred prevented him from ever mentioning the words.

Third, if there ever is a picture, it's to be painted by a fellowship-pable IFGN-DFSMC of the AB member above the age of account-ability—and the painter has to be male.

And right there the plow went under the root.

Ten years ago, four women of the Apostolic Believers Ladies' Tuesday Bible Symposium galumphed through a Gloria Steinem tome whose main goal was tub-thumping equality of the sexes. In an upper-middle to high dudgeon, the women raised their collective conscientiousness, lowered their collective horns, and charged T. Edsel.

The Good Pastor, facing a cash-flow problem of mastodonic proportions if the four women upgraded to Baptist, authorized the Apostolic Brethren to mutate to the Apostolic Believers. Doctrinally, he figured that if the initials stayed the same, well then, so did the theology.

As of now, The Great Baptistry Art Discussion has produced only a determination that the picture represent West Texas at its finest—as long as there are enough snow-covered mountains and cascading golden aspens.

But nothing even remotely resembling a "graven image" can be tolerated.

"Except maybe a dove."

"Naw, two doves, to represent marriage."

"No, three doves to symbolize the Trinity."

"Wait a minute, we cain't do that 'cause I've heard that the Catholics believe in the Trinity."

"Well, don't *you?*"

"I dunno. T. Edsel, do I believe in the Trinity?"

And so it goes.

The Major Prophets are being scrutinized in mind-numbing detail for guidance.

This week, T. Edsel and the Ladies' Tuesday Bible Symposium launched a year-long guided tour through the apocalyptic literature for apostolic example or necessary inference.

Meanwhile, the bare plaster with the lightning-shaped crack looms symbolically above the slime-rimmed lip of the baptistry.

Pity. Aspens are nice.

The Demons Amongst Us

It's taken a few days, but our free-form Church of the Apostolic Believers is back to normal, even though last Sunday's Adult Sunday School Class required a jumpstart for a few pacemakers.

Although Pastor T. Edsel Pedigrew, the sanctified guide for the intense, omni-directional flock of thirty-nine, has on occasion been point man in other spiritual tornadoes, this time it was Delmarine, his lumpish wife, who precipitated the crisis.

Last Sunday, T. Edsel, in the midst of his three-year cycle of touching on every verse in the Bible, found himself muttering through a crushingly dull lesson on the dietary laws of the ancient Hebrews. He listed the things that thou shalt not eat, and the apprehensive listeners finally relaxed when they realized they were prevented from eating only dry-land terrapins, camels, and turkey buzzards.

Sister Oliphant nodded righteously. "I can see how my ritual cleanliness would be messed up by a buzzard casserole."

Unfortunately, T. Edsel failed to notice Delmarine's increasing agitation. Her gaze wandered like a coon hunter's lantern, totally unable to fasten on anything solid. Finally, as T. Edsel allowed as how leaving off snake and horned toad should be enough of a sacrifice to balance out an occasional ham sandwich, Delmarine's quavering voice sliced through the comatose class with, "There's an evil demon living in our congregation."

Half the class heard it correctly, but thought they heard wrong. The other half also heard correctly, but wished they hadn't.

"Now, honey," T. Edsel said gently, "personally I can see the connection between your comment and the command not to eat a bat or a rattlesnake, but maybe you'd better elaborate a little bit more for the rest of the class."

Delmarine bit her lip as her eyes clouded up. "One member of our church family is controlled by a satanic power."

An older man bent forward, his face twisted with the battle between spiritual concern and raging curiosity. "Ummm, Sister Pedigrew, I know you don't want to call the person, but how long's this been goin' on?"

Delmarine dabbed at her eyes. "I've noticed it for about three months now. I just *know* everybody else has seen it, too."

The rest of the class leaned back, caught on the horns of wanting to nod wisely that they had, in fact, been on the verge of breaking the news themselves, and having to fight off the quizzical look that told the world they hadn't the foggiest notion who was riddled with infernal critters. A lot of throats were cleared and foreheads rubbed.

T. Edsel looked like he'd just swallowed some of that forbidden camel haunch. "Now, Delmarine, honey, I've got to know some of the symptoms of this demon possession."

"Everybody's seen it," Delmarine said with a shrug. "It's just everything the apostles talked about, like defying authority"—piercing gazes swept the room for telltale insolence—"screaming for absolutely no reason"—every mind flipped wildly through past worship services for uncontrolled howling—"and absolutely refusing to eat."

Squinting eyes and lightly shaken heads tried to make sense of the last statement. A fiendish spirit could obviously cause defying and bawling, but fasting seemed to come from an opposite motivation. T. Edsel licked his suddenly parched lips. "Delmarine, honey, just take your time and—"

"Don't 'honey' me!" Delmarine snapped. "Everybody here's seen it. They know it's right in my family."

Muttered asides choked behind gritted teeth. T. Edsel blanched to the color of a skinned catfish.

"They know it's little Roscoe Edsel, our son," she wailed into her hankie. "Roscoe's been defying my authority for at least three months, and a service doesn't go by without one of his screaming fits, and as for eating . . ."

The rest of the class leaned back, spiritual relief fighting with secular disappointment at a scabbed-over tragedy. Sister Oliphant leaned forward. "How old is your boy now, Delmarine?"

"Two years and three months."

Sage heads nodded and began exchanging shrill tribal wisdom concerning the Terrible Twos. It was a well-known and weekly reinforced concept that Roscoe Edsel, T. Edsel and Delmarine's youngest, was at least as headstrong as, and considerably more vocal than, his Daddy.

T. Edsel wisely signaled for the church secretary to scratch out any notes she had made. For the time being, their small band of Apostolic Believers could leave the Service of Exorcism on the shelf.

And that's a pity. T. Edsel has some colorful and innovative ideas on exorcism that would have played well to a Cedar Gap audience.

It's Always Been Like That

Just the other day, Pastor Pedigrew, both his integrity and craftiness intact, finally completed his twenty-four-month Project Facelift.

Just over two years ago, the Cedar Gap Independent Full Gospel Non-Denominational Four Square Missionarian Church of the Apostolic Believers began contemplating a sanctuary renovation. As the ranking scholar and fearless shepherd of the small congregation, T. Edsel prepared the preliminary sketches.

Then Delmarine, his triple-chinned wife, went to work with the Ladies' Tuesday Bible Symposium on the proposed changes.

"Changes?" a bright-eyed lady chirped. "Whattaya mean, changes! What's wrong with the way it's been since I joined back in '42?"

Delmarine tried to explain that the flaking paint above the pulpit gave the sanctuary a mildly leprous appearance, and while that was certainly Biblical, it did not bid one to come worship. "T. Edsel thought a nice muted blue-and-gray scheme would be comforting."

The announcement met with either stony squint-eyed staring or tight-lipped dissent. "Blue? What kind of blue? Are we talking sky, navy, azure, robin's-egg, electric, or what? I mean, I don't look good in every blue hue." The speaker fluffed her formerly gray hair. "Some colors clash."

"Well, I kinda like scarlet? Isn't that a religious color?"

"It was also the color on Hester's letter-jacket. Forget scarlet."

Blue alone ate up three Tuesday's symposia, not to mention the problems with ordering padded or unpadded seats.

"We're driftin', Brethren," a man in overalls said. "We're just gettin' too comfortable. There's somethin' in there about bein' at ease in Zion, ain't there, T. Edsel?"

But those were only surface ripples compared to the typhoon T. Edsel knew he would set off if he suggested rearranging the power sources at the front of the church. T. Edsel frowned at the auditorium situation and decided . . . the choir loft had to be moved.

Actually, "loft" was a tad presumptious. The seven women and two men in the Adult Sanctuary Choir sat in folding chairs behind a two-by-four railing off to the north side of the auditorium. The pulpit stand, a hand-fashioned creation rescued from a defunct traveling drama group performing *Elmer Gantry*, stood directly in the center of the small stage area.

T. Edsel quickly realized that although the symbolism inherent in a centrally positioned pulpit perfectly mirrored his theology, it messed up his master renovation plan. That stand had to move off to the south side of the sanctuary, both to balance the choir's relocated seats and to open up the view for the new baptistry painting he still envisioned.

"Brethren," T. Edsel said, his voice low enough for a TV anchorman, "we've got to keep the Great Trinity of Faith plainly visible."

"Now, Pastor Pedigrew," Sister Oliphant, the chairwoman of the Sanctuary Committee, said slowly, "by 'trinity' you mean—"

"Preachin', singin', an' baptizin', of course. The pulpit, the choir, and the baptistry, our three-sided keystone of Faith."

"Pastor, our pulpit has always been right there in the center, deviating neither to the left nor to the right." Sister Oliphant looked around, proud of her mishandling of scripture. "It's always been there in the middle, and it's gonna stay right there in the middle."

That was two years ago. Beginning that week, early every Monday morning, T. Edsel crept into the sanctuary, looked around warily for any stray Watchers or roving Holy Ones, then carefully nudged the pulpit stand one inch to the south. Then he fluffed up the telltale carpet and refocused the overhead floodlight.

Ninety weeks and ninety inches later, the migratory lumber arrived at the exact spot for balancing a choir loft. T. Edsel called a general meeting for that Sunday afternoon.

"I seem to remember, a couple a years ago, somebody suggested movin' the choir up on the pulpit area. For symbolic reasons, of course."

"Well, that'd be nice. That north wall has always looked sorta bare."

"Or, I just thought of another idea." T. Edsel played his trump. "We could leave the choir where it is, and move the pulpit stand over in the middle to balance the pulpit area."

Sister Oliphant, still chairwoman of the Sanctuary Committee, cleared her throat menacingly. "Sorry, we can't do that."

"What's the problem?"

"As long as I've been a member here, that pulpit's always been off to the south side, and it's gonna stay right there on the south side."

The nine-member choir is now up on the preacher's level, the cracked plaster looms symbolically behind the baptistry, and Pastor Pedigrew caroms his sermons in on his congregation from his new vantage point nearer the south wall.

That only proves that tradition is a wonderful thing and certainly more reliable than memory.

SATURDAY'S JOURNAL

THE GRAY COAT

ell, it's Saturday again in Cedar Gap. A gentle touch of cedar is riding the light breeze off the mesa. Two scissortails are curving and diving at moths. And a lot of people are remembring Anna Conrack.

Anna would have been eighty-two in another month. Hers was a good ending, the kind most of us want, with only three months for the downhill part and no pain. Her husband, Ned, died, oh, about forty years ago when Archie, their oldest, was just ready for college; then there was Betsy, Carl, and finally Deborah, their youngest, about ten. It was Anna's idea to name the kids alphabetically. Times were tough, money scarce, kids growing—and there was only Anna.

When the end finally came, the four gathered in the old family home for some decisions. "Look at this drawer full of pictures," Betsy said. "They must go back to when we were in grade school."

Carl picked up a small, much-handled snapshot. "Yeah, I was in third grade in this one. That's Archie's shirt I'm wearing."

"Huh," Deborah said, "that's Archie's shirt *I'm* wearing, too. Mama just kept cutting down shirts until they got to me, and I only got to hand them to the ragbag."

Archie, ruddy-faced and plump, gazed at the picture a long time. "Nah, both of those were Daddy's shirts first. All my stuff came from his closet."

The four stood quietly, thinking. "I didn't know that," Deborah said. "Mama must have been a tough lady, to see Daddy's shirts on us year after year."

Archie peered over the top of his spectacles. "You don't *know* tough. Mama practiced whippings on me, and by the time she got to you and Carl, all she could do was thump your knotty heads and give you cookies."

"You're talkin' like you been into Luther's private stock," Carl said. "*You* were always Mama's favorite, you and Deb."

"You're crazy!" Archie said.

"Aw, you *know* you were." Carl squinted into the gloom of the dusty bedroom. "The big strong older brother and the cute little baby sister."

"Stop it!" Betsy said, cutting off the argument with a wave of her hand. "That's not why we're here. The funeral home just called and needs to know if we've decided what kind of a dress to put on Mama."

Deborah, chubby and still sort of blond, pulled open a closet door thick with several generations of paint. "We can look in here for something, but the funeral director said they have some nice new ones with frills."

"Forget that," Carl snorted. "We can't bury Mama in something she never even wore. It just flat don't seem fittin'."

"Okay, okay," Deborah said defensively. "I was just presenting all the options."

Betsy moved hangers, then smiled. "Well, will you look at this! Here's Mama's old gray coat. Why in the world would she keep that?"

"How old is that coat, anyway?" Deborah asked, fingering the big plastic buttons.

"Older than you," Archie said. "We got a picture around here someplace of her bringing you home from the hospital, and I'm pretty sure she was wearing it then."

Betsy held up the hanger holding the limp gray coat. "She sure did like that coat. She just kept wearing it year after year. Seems like every time school opened, she said she couldn't find another coat that pleased her as much as this one."

Archie blinked, then gazed out the window. "You know, she always said that same thing just before she'd get something for one of us kids with what little money she had."

"I remember she said that when I needed a suit to go to college."

"You remember that pink graduation dress I got? She said the same thing then."

"She was about ready to get a new coat that time I needed a bicycle for my paper route."

"I can't remember Mama without this old gray coat. It even smells like her."

The four stood gazing at the coat and remembering. Finally, Betsy said quietly, "Then I guess it's settled."

The four of them received friends around the casket in Anna's old house with Anna dressed in her favorite gray coat. Everyone who saw her smiled, then related some incident when she came to church or PTA or Greenslope's Drugs pulling the kids and wearing that gray coat.

Plain, but with obvious quality, Anna and the coat formed a natural pair. It's only right they should go out together.

CHAPTER 9

THE FEARLESS MEDIA

OF CEDAR GAP

 *ou Just Ask "Dear Dolly"*

It's one thing to live in a city of a million and be completely dependent on the radio and TV for information. You feel a totally different reaction in Cedar Gap when you realize you can walk out the front door of the Palace Cafe, yell something, and know that at least a quarter of the town will hear you. Further, you know that within the hour, the other three-quarters of the population will have at least a close approximation of what you yelled.

Thus, Ann and Abby and Geraldo Rivera have a place in the social fabric of Cedar Gap, but that place is way down the taxonomy of important counseling sources. For your high-level Gestalt therapy and mind-bending biofeedback, the best sources—besides, of course, Luther Gravely on a roll—are Dolly Hooter's biweekly column in the *Cedar Gap Galaxy-Telegraph* and Murphy Gumpton's Saturday-morning call-in radio show.

We're not just talking entertainment; we're talking life-changing material. These are our local answers to Primal Scream Therapy.

It's been, oh, four or five years since Dolly kicked off her column, "Talk To Me!"—her soul-searching answers to Cedar Gapians' problems. Since research isn't Dolly's long suit, she tends to wing it.

Dear Dolly: My boy "Clyde" doesn't like high school. What can I do? Signed, Frustrated in Ballinger.

Dear Fruss: Look, just explain to "Clyde" (sure!) that for every grade below a B, he loses his car for one day every week, counting backwards from Saturday. Even if he's sorry in math, in no time at all he'll figure out that the only driving he'll be doing will be to church. If, however, he takes after his daddy and can't reason exactly straight, write me for another suggestion concerning a hoe handle, a rocky hillside, and a long hot afternoon.

However, personal concern has always been a hallmark of "Talk To Me!"

Dear Dolly: This is a terrible problem. I'm in love with two men, and I want to keep both of them. They both say they'll kill theirselves if I leave either one of them. What am I gonna do? Signed, Troubled in Cisco.

Dear Troubled: Listen, if those two eat a lot of egg-salad sandwiches and order those little green drinks with crushed ice and umbrellas sticking out of them, then you don't have what I'd call just a real substantial bargain. On the other hand, if you say both of those ol' boys stand real proud in their roping boots and they can't live without four-alarm chili and cool mountain mornings, then I'll just call you a liar to your anonymous face, because by this time if they were real men, one would have shot the other. Come on, serious up. I've got some people out there with real problems.

Since survival is a constant theme in West Texas, every column has what Dolly calls her Protectionist Consultation.

Dear Dolly: I live right at the bottom of a mesa, and the snakes are about to drive us to the city. What can we do? Signed, Scairt in Baird.

Dear Scairt: Go get yourself a pair of beady-eyed guinea hens and an old cat that's as mean as four pounds of chopped liver. Trust me, snakes won't live around either of them. Of course, one may kill the other, but I guarantee you'll be snake-free.

One desperate cry for help just appeared through the mail slot at the *Galaxy-Telegraph.*

Dear Dolly: Help! I can't get a date anywheres. All the men are either married, work shift-work, or chew Red Man Plug. I mean, we're talking about an arid, smelly wasteland out there. Signed, Desperate in the West.

Dear Desperate: I think your main problem is attitude. You've been waiting around too long for an accountant wearing Reeboks and a shirt with some endangered species printed on the pocket. Wrooooooong! You just come on down to the paper, I'll get my best little Monkey-Ward party dress, and we'll team up with Butch and Buster and No-Neck and go honky-tonking. Loosen up, Des!

About a month ago, Dolly got an anonymous letter from a confused rigger, written on a piece of a Piggly-Wiggly grocery sack.

Dear Dolly: Since things are tough in the oil patch here in Texas, I'm thinking about taking a roughnecking job in the Near East. Whattaya think? Signed, Alive but Broke.

Dear Mr. Broke: You've got some real high-quality thinking going for you there, Dummy! You mean you'd voluntarily move to some low-rent camel-eating country smaller than a panhandle ranch so you could work for a sunburned idiot in shades and a bathrobe who uses two shoelaces to hold a towel on his head?

That would certainly get ME to leave West Texas! You get three
of those toad-brained squiggle-writers together and all they can
agree on is that two of them will eventually mug the third. Tell
you what, go up on our mesa and bed down with the rattlers
and scorpions without air conditioning or TV or a convenience
store for about a month. If you like that, then you'll like working for the nerd in the bathrobe. Sheesh!

As Dolly says constantly, "Ya gotta get right on down to the
source of the problem." A slow, suppressed boil was never her style.
My own favorite answer was to a lady up in Jones County.

*Dear Dolly: My daughter's marrying a boy who dropped out of high
school to work on his car. What can I do about that jerk? Signed,
Concerned Mother.*

Dear Con: WHICH jerk?

Keep those cards and letters coming. Wisdom is alive and well and
living in Cedar Gap.

Gumpton's Call-in Show

And if your arthritis is kicking up so you can't hold a pencil, then
you can dial up "I Hear Ya Talkin'," Murphy Gumpton's call-in show
on KCDR-FM, our little 250-watt station upstairs in a back room
of the Palace Hotel. Murph's standard Saturday format is to have a
local expert sit with him and field calls from listeners.

His worst show was when Wellington Thorn, the U.S. Senator
from Texas, stopped off during his last campaign. The poor sap's
from a suburb of Dallas, and not only does he not know very much,
he doesn't even suspect most things. His hour of smudged answers
only proves what's been said for two terms: Like a brain-damaged
goose, he wakes up on a different planet every day.

On the other hand, everybody remembers the show aired during
the last presidential election when Murphy, a wild-eyed Trumanite

Democrat, invited Sybil Jorgenson, our most fanatical GOP funda-
mentalist, to share the mike. The phone never stopped ringing for
the entire program, but not once was it answered. For the full hour,
Murph and Sybil leaned in nose-to-nose, shouting, accusing, and
finger-wiggling, with Sybil being characterized as having the arche-
typical Republican inability to roll a rock down a steep hill, and
Murphy being told that if he had the brains of a Democratic buzzard,
he'd probably fly backwards.

Last Saturday, Murph invited Waldo Beeler, the owner of Beeler's
Fine Used Trucks and Tractors, to be the visiting expert.

"We're gonna talk today about the burgeoning transportation in-
dustry in Cedar Gap. Whoops! Waldo, there's your first call."

"Hey, Waldo, what kinda car you drive?"

"Murrican. Only it's a truck, not a car. 'Member, now, this is
Texas. You got another question?"

"Yeah. What's the first thing you look for in a truck?"

"Same thing as in a woman—dependability over the long haul.
Course, you tend to find it more in trucks than women, plus you can
trade trucks in a bunch easier. Might keep that in mind the next time
you acquire either one." A long patch of dead air ensued. "Uh, I uz
just funnin' there, hon. Now, don't go takin' it personal, sugar. I'll
explain over lunch. Scuse me, I got another call."

"Hey, Waldo, you'd probably sell more trucks if you washed 'em
occasionally. Or, are you savin' Cedar Gap water?"

"I know that voice! Now, lookee here, Leonard, Beeler's Fine
Used Trucks and Tractors is as ecologically aware a firm as exists.
Howsomever, my trucks—an' yourn, too—don't always benefit
from too much water an' scrubbin'."

"You mean dirt's good for 'em?"

"Show me a clean mechanic, an' I'll show you a sorry mechanic.
Same for a truck. If it ain't been where the dirt is, it ain't been where
the work is. 'Sides, just like a man, some ground-in dirt an' a few
bumps shows they got character."

"I don't know, Waldo, my truck's kindly new, an' I don't feel like
workin' it over with a sticka stovewood just to make it look proper."

"Aw, they's several other things you can do. Get yourself a bale a
cheap straw an' some empty oilcans an' thow 'em in the back. The

straw'll smell good in the sun, an' the cans'll make a real nice work-manlike clatter when ya turn corners. An' leave a couple a feed sacks showin'. That'll prove to folks you're serious about gettin' out an' gettin' under when trouble comes. Gotta go, there's another call."

"Hey, Waldo, I'm thinkin' about gettin' a pair a them little square lights for my truck, but I think I need somethin' else to pretty it up an' tell people I'm a serious driver."

"Tell you what, friend, come on down to my lot, an' I'll give you a free bumper sticker that says *Keep Texas Beautiful; Buy a Yankee a Ticket to Cleveland*. By the way, have you got one a them screen-wire sunshades for your back window with a picture of an armadillo or a twelve-point buck on it? An' speakin' a armadillos, you'll need a little plastic one to hang from your rear-view mirror. Course, I'm sure you already got a gunrack an' a lever-action Winchester up in your back window."

A long silence. "You know, Waldo, there's some places won't allow guns out in the open like that."

"Naw! Whur?"

"Chicago, for one place, an' New York City for another."

Waldo ignored the open mike as he mulled it over.

"Well, it's like I always said." He slurped some coffee. "Them big cities ain't ready for civilization."

SATURDAY'S JOURNAL

THE TALE OF A WING

nd Saturday being come, there was great rejoicing in the village of Gap-in-the-Cedar. Although, forsooth, to keep this journal truly straightened, one paire of citizens, an honest nobleman and his woman, were gooseless. And therein lies this tale of a wing.

It was of a Tuesday, last, when Lord Morton, of the House of Barstow, spake to his woman, Ora-of-the-Stern-Countenance. "As thou knowest, my lady, the Feaste of Saint Buster approacheth wherein we celebrate the patron saint of our village with a communal banquet."

"Aye, I have the feaste planned, husband. Rememberest thou that fat goose our Lord Mayor braggest about?"

Lord Morton, not averse to an occasional celebratory libation, hiccuped loudly. "Aaaaah, yes, our mayor, Yancy, son of Whirter. His goose crop, to hear him, exceeds that of all others as Dallastown exceeds our Gap-in-the-Cedar."

"Verily, thou hast it," Lady Ora said slowly, eyeing the receding level of her husband's goblet. "Canst thou be trusted to betake thyself to McWhirter's goosefarm and choose this communal gifte?"

"Woman," Lord Morton said loudly, "my family's famed flair for finding fitting fine fowl has fallen fairly for four hundred . . ." Lord Morton, his storehouse of *f* words exhausted, frowned against a multiplying headache.

Lady Ora gazed owlishly at the slurred statement. "Then hie thee to get that prize goose, ere I am reduced to preparing an embarrassing pottage."

Solidly fortified against both freezing and snakebite, Lord Morton of Barstow staggered into the gloaming toward the malodorous and noisy goosefarm of the robust Squire Yancy.

"Hail, good citizen," Squire Yancy harrumphed. "Why art thou afield so late of a dark evening?"

Lord Morton kicked at a goose pecking at his brogans. "Because I fain would purchase—get away, goose, ere I stomp thee into liver paste—would purchase the best example of thy feathered stock."

"Aye, that would be the great goose that ruleth my fowlyard." Sir Yancy peered at Lord Morton's rocking motion and bloodshot eyes. "Wouldst thou take it this eve, or wouldst the morn seem fairer—when thy fabled keen vision is restored?"

Lord Morton, bellicose when unduly influenced by sloshing spirits, gritted his teeth. "Thy concern is misplaced, neighbor Yancy." He pulled unsteadily at his coin bag. "Name thy price."

"Five pieces of silver," the son of Whirter said, "but remember, ere thou lettest the bird go, thou must cut the end of its wingfeathers, else it will betake itself to the aire an' fly to distant climes."

"Here," Lord Morton said huffily, "is thy goose's ransom. Now, tell me, pray, why must the feathers be trimmed thus?"

"No one knoweth for sure, Lord Morton," Squire Yancy whispered, "but there is talk of a witches' conspiracy. What we do know is that with the wings equal, the goose can fly, whereas with a few feathers shortened by the width of three fingers, it will flop around like a gaffed sturgeon." The Lord Mayor bit on a silverpiece. "Forget not the trimming."

On his careening stagger back to his manse, Lord Morton pulled and pinched at the feathers of the squawking bird's right wing until it resembled an unraveled jerkin. The goose, taking considerable exception to the trimming, nipped Lord Morton's ears and fingers until they matched the rosy hue of his nose. Finally home, the titular head of the House of Barstow threw the goose into a pen and staggered up to his room.

"Husband, didst thou obtain the bird?" Lady Ora was answered by a loud belch and a miscellaneous series of profanities concerning the long, iniquitous history of geese and their probable location in the afterlife. "Then, didst thou . . . of course he didn't," she muttered as she grabbed a knife and strode into the night air.

With a few quick strokes, she trimmed the protruding feathers on the goose's left wing. Unfortunately, in the dim moon's light, she missed the fact that she modified the longer wing, the one not tucked safely away from human grasping. The truncated bird, no longer the embarrassed owner of one long and one short wing, flapped tentatively. Then, with a totally ungooselike grin, it strained itself into the air to begin a long, honking glide toward the Great Mexican Ocean.

The chronicles are silent as to the next day's conversation between Lord Morton of Barstow and Lady Ora-of-the-Stern-Countenance. Yea, we fair would give good money or provender to reproduce their visages when they spied a huge goose, toasted golden, carried by a young page from beyond our mesa. When asked concerning it, the page said mystically, "It appeared on two ragged wings as a miraculous gifte from Saint Buster."

Thus endeth the tale of a wing. Or should it be a wing and a prayer? Possibly, it was. . . . But hark, the feaste beginneth.

CHAPTER 10

VISITORS TO THE GAP

*he Dynamite Snapper Caper*

Cedar Gap has a bit of a geographical problem: It's a quarter of a mile up a more or less dead-end road. When they put the new San Antonio highway through back in the fifties, Cedar Gap was left high and dry on an unused piece of road, one end of which was eventually allowed to deteriorate, effectively keeping out most accidental visitors and strays.

However, not all strays pass us by. We're still sorting out our feelings about the day the "snapper" in his old panel truck drifted up to the curb fronting the Palace Cafe.

A tousled, bent man eased out of the dented truck. He nodded curtly to Lester Goodrich and Waldo Beeler. Lester nodded back. "Mornin'. Can we help ya?" Lester said.

The man scratched a wisp of gray mustache. "Might." He squinted up the street. "Reckon anybody needs some advertisin' fixed? I'm a snapper."

Lester cleared his throat. "Snapper. Don't know the word."

"Sign painter. Actually, I'm what they call a dynamite snapper." The man didn't even look at them; he'd explained before. "I specialize in black, red, and gold."

"Colors on a dynamite stick," Waldo said.

The man raised his eyebrows in appreciation of Waldo's erudition. "I see the Fontainebleau Beauty Spa's sign's homemade. A lady run it?"

Lester nodded. "Yeah. Corinne Iverson. But she's not much for upgradin'."

"I'll try, anyways." The man pulled a paint-splattered wooden box from the back of his panel truck. "I'm obliged for the name."

A few minutes later, Lester and Waldo watched Corinne's hand-lettered window sign disappear to a scraping razor blade. Then, slowly, like a sunset's change, a smaller sign blossomed in the center of the large window. Elegant lettering entwined in rose vines gently circled a misty French château.

As the snapper stepped outside for a final check, a preschooler pulling a red wagon stopped, fascinated by the brilliant colors. "Whatcher name, son?"

The boy kept gazing at the sparkling new sign. "Junior."

The snapper dipped a brush in a streaked bottle. With a few graceful strokes, he wrote *Junior* on the wagon. A smaller brush shaded in gold accents. The boy's eyes widened. "Don't touch it till lunch." Then the man picked up his snapper's box and walked toward Greenslope's Drugs, Notions and Hardware.

The peeling sign on Oliver Greenslope's front store-window disappeared to the same razor blade. Children just out of school sat cross-legged on the sidewalk, watching a delicate filigree appear, outlining the window, then bold black and red letters edged in gold fill in the main portion of the window.

The snapper squinted at the half-dozen kids. He walked outside. "Anybody got an A for an initial?" A tiny girl in pigtails raised her hand tentatively. "Let me see your notebook." A few circular strokes of a pen outlined an elaborate letter A behind a delicate, smiling pigtailed head.

"Hey, Annie," a boy marveled, "that's *you* he's drawin' in your book." The boy hesitated, the traditional fear in the presence of talent battling with the possibility of a one-of-a-kind treasure. "Mister, can you do a C, for *Carl*?"

Without a change of expression, the man reached for Carl's notebook. In less than a minute, the boy's square-faced, big-eared likeness appeared, smiling out of a shaded block C. Immediately, the rest of the children crowded around, schoolbooks and scraps of paper thrust out.

The man glanced up. A gray sedan eased across Main Street, the telltale star on the door catching the glint of the setting sun. The snapper quickly finished the last drawing. A few minutes later, the old panel truck coughed to life, circled the block slowly, then disappeared.

"That snapper sure didn't talk much," Waldo muttered. "I'd like to know more about what he does."

Deputy Sheriff Donnie Sue Kingsbury leaned against the pecan tree shading the cafe door. "What didn't talk much?"

"He called himself a snapper, said that meant a sign painter." Waldo nodded at the new Fontainebleau sign.

Donnie Sue smiled broadly. "Well, look at that! Where'd you say he came from?"

"Don't know," Lester said. "He just drove in, painted two windows, talked to some kids, then left about—well, about the time you showed up."

"Kids?" Donnie Sue said, frowning. "What kids?"

"Those up yonder."

"I'll be back in a minute. Don't leave."

That was Tuesday. The whole town's talking about what might have happened to the children, that at the minimum he's an escaped Communist or Satan-worshiper, and of the 256 people in Cedar Gap, at least 400 saw him clearly.

But they didn't see Annie. Tuesday, at supper, she kept quiet while her parents talked excitedly about the man called the snapper. "Terrible name." "Prob'ly another nickname for kidsnapper." "I figure he's gotta be a serial murderer."

Later, long after she was supposed to be asleep, Annie sat cross-legged on her bed, mesmerized at her drawing of a capital A framing a face with graceful braids and laughing eyes. Then she smiled, kissed the picture, and hid it in a shoebox marked *My Treasures*.

He Was Just a Good Hand

A fair number of our Gapians are permanent fixtures. We know their peculiarities and druthers, which helps us work around them. Most of these people were born either in town or near here and manage to stay despite the problems.

On the other hand, we do get an occasional visitor. Right now, we're one citizen shy of where we were last week. He was a temporary citizen, but one of us nonetheless.

We're not sure of his real name. We called him *Yank* because when we asked him where he was from, he just muttered, "Up north."

He stepped into the Palace Cafe about a month ago, squinting against the sudden shade, obviously looking for something. His Levi's were worn but clean, his face sharp enough to chop wood with. The lean body was forty, but the eyes were twice that. Brenda Beth glanced up. "Lookin' for somethin'?"

"Work." His glance swept the cafe. "There's usually a bulletin board around somewhere, asking for a good hand."

"There's not much extra work right now, but you could talk to Morton Barstow over there by the window. I heard he might work some fences."

Yank tightened Morton's fences for a week, then painted Sybil Jorgenson's garage, cleaned a henhouse, split firewood on shares, and picked up aluminum cans along the highway. And every Friday, he bought a money order from Bertie Faye Hogg, our postmistress.

"Every week's the same," Bertie Faye stage-whispered, her hands acting out the full scene. "He puts all his money on the table, divides it into equal piles, then buys a money order with one pile."

"Where's he send it?"

Bertie Faye's chubby face glowed with her secret knowledge. "A post-office box in Buffalo, South Dakota. I looked it up. It's about the size of Cedar Gap." She sat back, her triumph complete.

Somebody whistled. "What's he doin' down here?"

Nobody wanted to say it, but finally somebody did. "Running." Several people nodded imperceptibly.

"Reckon he's dangerous?"

"Don't seem to be," Morton said. "He's sleeping in Ambrosio's old camping trailer. He bought Ambrosio's kids some candy once, then hid and watched 'em eat it."

Eyebrows went up. That put a new dimension to Yank's problem. He's a family man. And he's lonely.

Nobody said a thing. There were no plans, no group decision, just a bunch of people suddenly aware of a tender mind.

Yancy McWhirter let it drop in Yank's presence that his wife had some extra stew he'd "be proud to see eaten up, so's I don't have to stare at it all next week." It was no accident that Yancy's house also smelled like biscuits and Lemon Pledge.

The next day, Zaccheus Tatum took his two kids over to drop off half an angel food cake at Yank's trailer, then sat and ate it with him.

Tuesday, T. Edsel Pedigrew, the preacher down at the Church of the Apostolic Believers, hired Yank to paint a storeroom adjacent to the monthly luncheon by the Ladies' Tuesday Bible Symposium. The smell of talcum powder, hymnbooks, and casseroles flooded the place.

Wednesday, Ferrell Epperson employed Yank for a full day of cutting weeds around the elementary school where he looked up a lot to watch children laugh and play. Vera Frudenburg, our ace third-grade teacher, invited him in for the Pledge of Allegiance and lunch, "if you can stand the sound of healthy kids."

That same night, Eldred Simpson, pastor of the First Baptist Church of Cedar Gap, happened onto Yank eating alone at the Palace Cafe. "Sir," Eldred said, "I'd consider it a great favor if you'd take a look at my garage and advise me about a new roof. As a swap, I'd be pleased to share some newly cranked ice cream." Eldred neglected to mention that his backyard lies directly under the open windows where the choir was practicing some old hymns for a Founders' Day service.

"I think it was someplace in the third verse of 'Sweet Bye and Bye,' about where the women sang 'For the blessings that hallow our days.' The man got up, and in a husky voice asked if I was good for one last bit of help.

"'It's part of my job description,' I said. I asked him what he needed.

"'A lift to the Abilene Bus Station.' He bought a one-way ticket to Buffalo, South Dakota."

We never learned his name, or why he was away from his family. Maybe it was cowardice, or his wife hated him, or he couldn't find work in Buffalo. It didn't really matter. He was a good hand, and in Cedar Gap that means something.

Yank once said that's what his daddy was, a good hand, and that's all he wanted to be—a hired hand who gave good work for wages.

There are worse things that could go on a tombstone.

Oh, yeah, there are a lot worse things that could decorate a final resting-place. Things like

HE NEVER TOOK HIS KIDS TO CHURCH

or

SHE COULDN'T LEARN TO BAKE BISCUITS

or

HE SCRATCHED ON THE BREAK

Don't Never Scratch on the Break

We've got this old beat-up pool table in the back of the Palace Hotel and Cafe that's almost always busy. We'd like to have a regulation poolhall with a fluorescent hanging light, an animated Coors Beer sign, and a smelly rest room that says Men Only, but in a town of 256 souls—most of them church-going traditionalists—a genuine poolhall would stand out like Oreos at a church picnic.

Of course, that's just an excuse we use. As much as anything, we don't have a poolhall because we don't have any genuine glowering, pack-of-Luckies-rolled-up-in-a-T-shirt-sleeve kind of pool players.

We've got too many like Yancy McWhirter, our seventy-four-year-old mayor who, in bright sunlight, has trouble lining up the chalk with the cue tip.

Or Stafford Higginbotham, who runs Hig's Propane Service.

Hig's so nervous from working around that big tank of explosive liquid that his trembling fingers blur like a hummingbird's wings.

Or Luther Gravely, who keeps asking which ball to focus on. "Line up the middle white one," somebody said. He did, and splattered Hig's spit cup all over the Rotarian's gum machine.

Part of the problem is the oldest rule in pool: Don't never scratch on the break. Ever. Living down that sort of gaffe takes not years but generations. "You 'member Everett Baill, from over at Brownwood?" "Naw, I don't mind no Baills from Brownwood." "Sure you do! It was his uncle Mort who scratched that time on the break back in '64." "Aw, *that* useless bunch of Baills!"

You learn young to aim true on the break in Cedar Gap.

But there are exceptions. Ten-year-old boys. Luther Gravely. And visitors.

Two days ago, a huge flatbed truck broke down out on the highway. The hum of talking and kitchen noise dipped to cathedral silence when the trucker strutted into the Palace. His arms resembled cured hams poking out of a sleeveless *Dead Animals World Rock Tour* sweatshirt. He'd washed his hair the day Nixon resigned and figured that took care of it.

He frowned at the menu. "Is this jalapeno barbecue worth eating?" He pronounced it "juh-LAPP-uh-no." And then he sneered.

Brenda Beth Kollwood, the Palace's owner-manager and waitress, is so walleyed she can't focus on anything nearer than Dallas, but she could tell the driver needed an education. "I'm told by those who are supposed to know that it's a tad warm."

"Well, gimme some, an' if it's not too weak, I'll take some home to my baby sister."

Brenda Beth just smirked as she wrote up the order. She walked into a broom closet, picked six tiny dried peppers the size of pencil erasers off a hanging bush, and ground them into a plate of the Palace Cafe's best barbecue.

The trucker was on his second bite before the first one took effect. You've got to give him his due—he didn't flinch. His eyes squinched almost shut as he drained a whole trembling thirty-two-ounce glass of ice tea. He sucked in and huffed out air, trying desperately to cool his inflamed mouth.

About that time, his appetite left him. His tear-filled eyes spotted what he thought was an escape through the poolhall, but he couldn't know there's no back door in the poolhall. He blinked through blurred eyes at the men standing quietly. To keep from looking even more foolish, he walked to the cue rack and picked up the brightest-colored cue, then growled, "Rack 'em." He couldn't see that the cue tip was warped—which was the reason the cue was painted in the first place.

The seven or eight men in the room at the time tried to look busy. Another dozen or so in a hunched-up line out into the cafe were real quiet, watching. The trucker blinked, then blinked again in a useless try at seeing through the tears. Then he grunted and shoved.

The warped cue glanced off the bottom of the cue ball and ripped a gaping hole in the green cloth. The cue ball, now airborne, caromed over the entire table and smashed the Rotarian's gum machine.

The silence was that of a monastery at midnight. A bit of asthmatic breathing, a swallowed dip whose owner would rather choke than move, a humming bee.

The trucker squinted at the torn felt like a dermatologist examining a new kind of wart. He sucked in and huffed a couple of times, then carefully peeled five twenties off a roll of bills, threw them on the pool table, and strutted out of our lives.

Luther, who was just sober enough not to laugh, nodded and said, "If y'all want me to, I can get ever' one of us three hours of graduate credit at A&M for what we just seen."

"What kinda class, Luther?"

"Seminar in Abnormal Behavior."

Only then did the laughter explode.

SATURDAY'S JOURNAL

THE GREAT CEDAR GAP

POWDER EXPLOSION

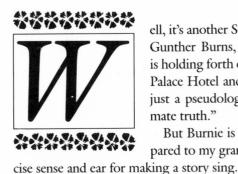

ell, it's another Saturday in Cedar Gap, and Gunther Burns, our premier tale-spinner, is holding forth on the old pew outside the Palace Hotel and Cafe. As he tells it, "I'm just a pseudologist searching for the ultimate truth."

But Burnie is a beardless beginner compared to my grandpap, a purist with a precise sense and ear for making a story sing.

Like the time back in the twenties when Mort Watkins tried to blow up the Cedar Gap General Store.

"That old store was long and narrow like a gun barrel," Grandpap used to tell us grandkids. "Shelves and glass-topped cases left a thin little cluttered aisle right down the middle of the store, with a clearing for the old potbellied stove, a rick of stovewood, and three or four chairs. In bad weather, you could always find a buncha men around the stove, whittlin', cussin' a little, tellin' stories about how many eight-point deer they'd spotted or how many cords of wood they'd cut as a boy."

Here Grandpap always looked at the ceiling and pointed at imaginary men. "There was Charley Jones, then Bill Riggs, and Ray

Littlepage. Jess Bailey, old man Bailey's not-very-bright boy, got a place on the kindling. Hobart Lyles, the runt of the bunch, and old Oliver Rutherford sat on nail kegs. Oliver's peg leg was a souvenir from the last battle of the Big War. And somebody else, but I disremember who.

"Anyway, Mort Watkins walked in. Everybody howdied him, but Mort looked put out about something. He picked up a coupla things, put them down, then walked over to Chester Bosley, who owned the store.

"'Gimme ten pounds of gunpowder.' Everything got real quiet. Ten pounds of gunpowder could blow Cedar Gap halfway to Houston.

"Chester frowned. 'That's a lotta powder.'

"Mort picked up the can of powder kinda careless-like. 'Yeah, a whole lot. You'll get your money when my cow drops her calf.'

"Ches never moved. 'What if you lose that calf? Do I still get my money?'

"'You ever lost any money on me before?'

"'You never owed this much before.'

"'I gotta have this powder to blast out some stumps.'

"'Let the stumps wait till the calf comes.'

"'I want the stumps out *now*.' Both were talking louder and louder.

"'You're sayin' that you want the stumps out and that I can just wait for my money.'

"All this time, Mort kept pushing the powder can back and forth on the counter. 'Yeah, that's the way I see it.'

"Chester snarled, 'That's about what I'd expect from a Watkins.'

"Mort slammed his fist on the counter and yelled, 'I ain't gonna listen to any more of your insults!' With that, he jumped at the counter, grabbed the powder can, and chunked it in the stove.

"Well, that split it," Grandpap said. "Jess wasn't so shy of brains but what he could run from burning powder, so he fetched a lunge that scattered stovewood ever' which way.

"Everybody was on the far side of the stove from the front door, so they naturally headed out back. Oliver's wooden leg rolled on a log, and he sat down ka-smash and broke that peg right in two. He laid there and squalled as everybody tromped all over him.

"But the back door was still locked from the night before. Everybody yelled as they looked at the high window, then at the stove, then at the front door. They figured real quick it was either go by the stove or blow up, so Jess fetched another lunge, slipped on more stovewood, tromped on Oliver again, and ran screaming clear to his farm. Hobart Lyles was a little bitty feller, but he clutched a two-hundred-pound sack of salt in front of him as he stumbled by the stove, yellin', 'Watch it! Watch it! Watch it!' Oliver screeched a machine-gun prayer outlining his unqualified desire to leave immediately to go missionarying to the Patagonians.

"Well, Ray finally saw Mort and Chester crouched behind the piece goods laughing, so he quit jumping for the back window and dug the powder can outta the stove. It was full of sawdust.

"Hobart Lyles got three men to help him carry the sack of salt back in the store, and somebody yelled at deaf old Oliver, who began fifteen minutes of nonrepetitive cussing."

I remember asking Grandpap, "Where were you when all of this happened?"

"Aw, you know how stories are. You forget where you heard 'em." He paused and grinned slyly at us. "But I sure wish I could remember who that other feller was."

All of us grinned back. All of us knew.

CHAPTER 11

THE ANIMALS OF CEDAR GAP

hose Dogs of Cedar Gap

The other day, part of the predictable scenery in the Palace Cafe changed locations. Instead of sitting off in a corner quaffing at a straw sticking out of his inside coat pocket, Luther Gravely slouched over a yellow legal pad and slugged back coffee strong enough to trot a gopher across as he squinted against a headache with a half-life of about thirty years.

Brenda Beth Kollwood, the Palace Cafe's best waitress, shushed a noisy table. "Luther's working on an article for a magazine."

"No kiddin'," someone yelled. "What's it about, Luther?"

Luther flinched at the shout. "Dogs," he whispered.

A murky silence oozed through the cafe. "Dogs?" someone muttered.

"Quit yellin'. Yeah, dogs. You amateurs probably never noticed it, but we got more kinds of dogs in Cedar Gap than any place in the world."

"I only know two kinds," Arnold Curnutt said. "The kind you hunt with and the kind you throw rocks at."

Luther winced at the sound of a dropped cup. "You people lack the scientific eye we trained psychologists have. Just look outside right now at that dog swagger. If that ain't John Wayne, I've never seen it." Everyone jostled for a glimpse of a squatty dog lumbering across Main Street. "Is that The Duke lookin' for a fight, or what?"

"Naw," Arnold said, "that's Waldo Beeler's arthritic ol' bulldog. He's just like Waldo—if he ain't struttin', he ain't movin'."

"Well, there's my article! Dogs and humans that get together not only act like each other; they wind up lookin' like each other as well."

"Now, wait a minute!" Yancy McWhirter, our seventy-four-year-old mayor, sat up. "You sayin' that me an' my ol' Labrador look alike?"

Everybody peered at Yancy in a new light. Eyes squinted and mouths pursed. "Well, now that you mention it, Yancy, if you'd just part your hair on the other side . . ." "Ya know, Yancy, I was watchin' you two walkin' away from me the other day, an' with the light behind you . . ."

Luther held up his pen hand. "You remember that Great Dane Edgar Allen Plymate had down at Winters? That dog started out mean as Hitler, but Edgar Allen began feeding him table scraps, and the longer they ate the same food, the more they looked alike. Right now, that dog is as mellow as pond-water, and it's a race between 'em to see who gets to three hundred pounds first."

"Hey, Luther, you may be onto somethin'. Remember that ol' sheepdog of yours? Mac something-or-other, wasn't it?"

Luther turned slowly, a frown creasing his forehead. "It was MacTavish, and let's just forget him. We got other dogs here in—"

"Yeah! I remember ol' MacTavish. His bark always seemed sorta slurred."

Luther and MacTavish had several other similarities. Their gaze had the same fuzzy lack of focus. Both of them had a breath that would kill Johnson grass. And both jumped and snarled at loud noises.

Luther's still touchy about that hound. MacTavish was a pretty good dog, but Luther bragged so much about the dog's sheephandling ability he backed himself into a corner; it was either enter MacTavish in a sheepdog competition, or go suck eggs.

In a sure-nuff sheepdog contest, the handler controls his dog by a series of whistles or hand motions, with the goal being to move four sheep from a distant pasture up into a pen near the judges.

MacTavish did well the first two rounds, and only lost a couple of points for biting one judge who sneezed unexpectedly. Unfortunately, Luther began celebrating the third round a bit early. His quart of warm homemade margaritas began melting strategic muscles. First, he mixed up his arm signals, and when his lips turned into Silly Putty, his signal whistles began resembling a loose patch on a bicycle tube.

MacTavish, bewildered at the garbled signals from his master, zigzagged erratically across the pasture, doing his best to control the poor confused sheep. But after the fifth incoherent whistle, MacTavish snarled at the bleating sheep, turned his back cryptically, and headed for Nova Scotia where a sheepdog can get some respect. He never came back.

Several people mentioned MacTavish, but Luther's article already lay wadded on the floor.

"Arncha gonna write your dog story, Luther?"

Luther shook his head carefully. "Got a better idea. I'm doin' one on the group tragedy that comes when a town turns on its only intellectual."

It took four cups of coffee and enough unwarranted praise for a Kiwanis convention to jumpstart the dog story. The alternative was too fierce to contemplate.

The Conversion of Attila the Hound

One morning a couple of years ago, Lester Goodrich walked out to get his mail and found a half-starved pup huddled by his mailbox. The tiny gray animal shivered in the high weeds until Lester reached for it.

"That pup weren't no bigger than your fist, and about half dead to boot," Lester said, "but it snarled and snapped like an alligator ever' time I went for it."

Lester named the pup Attila the Hound. It took over his yard, then his block, and finally the whole town, which included intimidating a Doberman three times his size. "That dog ain't big, but he demands an abnormal amount of daylight between him and the rest of the world. You get closer'n about as far as you can spit, and you'd better get used to walkin' on one leg cause ol' Attila'll have the other'n for lunch."

It's not that Attila goes looking for trouble; his happiness just requires an anxiety-free environment. Objects from the mineral or vegetable kingdom are welcome in his vicinity, but animate objects possess a high probability of winding up as sushi. Size or shape has never been a variable to Attila. If it moved, it died, including the biggest rattler ever seen in Cedar Gap.

"Except he don't bother kids," Lester explained, "or adults who don't look at him too long," which is difficult for most adults, because Attila is as nonstandard as a dog can get and not be a coyote. You just naturally stare at a gray-speckled animal that slinks rather than runs, screeches instead of barking, and has black holes where eyes should be.

We're talking about one intimidating animal. Or he was until last Monday, when Treesie May Burkhalter, Carter Burkhalter's six-year-old granddaughter, brought her brain-damaged cat to town.

All Carter can do is shake his head. "About six months ago, Queen Victoria—that's the cat's name—was stalkin' a mouse in my wheatfield, an' I ran over her with my combine."

"Hurt pretty bad, was it?"

"Naw, the combine's fine. All I had to do was replace—"

"I meant the cat!"

"Oh . . . well, it was awful mangled. If Treesie May hadn't squalled so much, I'da put that ol' cat outta its misery. As it was, I helped a vet send his kid to college, an' just to save a three-legged one-eyed cat with half its brain gone." Carter spread his hands in frustration. "You've seen the cat. Whattaya think?"

Queen Victoria's most pressing problem concerns information retrieval and processing. If she heads for a saucer of milk, she loops out to the right with a series of spirals like a lopsided Frisbee. Since her aim isn't too keen, she'll get in the general vicinity of the milk, then roll over and over until she bumps up against the saucer. It's not the most efficient means of travel. Plus, the head injury shorted out her vocal mechanism, so instead of meowing, Queen Victoria chirps. Like a bird. It's unnerving.

Last Monday, Treesie May came skipping and singing down Main Street, with Queen Victoria looped over her arm. Suddenly tired of the bouncing ride, the cat squirmed and flopped away.

The movement caught Attila's eye. With the precise aim of a cruise missile, the dog homed in on Queen Victoria. He was a breath and a snap away when the cat sat back on its good hind leg, blinked its remaining eye, and warbled like an oriole.

Attila skidded and stumbled past the furry apparition, which started on one of its rotary search-and-destroy missions. Attila opened his mouth either to yelp or growl, but the cat kept circling under his muzzle.

For a full ten minutes, Attila the Hound watched Queen Victoria's spiraling stagger. Then, without so much as a whimper, he nudged the cat into a more or less straight line toward his own home in the back of Lester's garage.

"That cat ain't worth skinnin' for fish bait," Lester muttered. "Course, it don't cost nothin' either, 'cause ol' Attila forages for the both of 'em. It's sorta like the dog needed either a hobby or a toy. He just lays around an' watches the cat go in circles." Lester grinned. "Course, for sure that cat's funny to watch. Maybe that's why Attila puts up with it."

Everybody in the Palace Cafe nodded. We've got a couple of people like that in Cedar Gap. Naturally, nobody put names to them.

Revenge of the Furball

A poet once suggested that when you bait a mousetrap with cheese, it's usually best to leave some room for the mouse. Simply put, it means that planning ahead saves problems. To use another humble homily, camping out is more fun when it's voluntary. You're wondering how those fit together? Just listen up.

Gunther Burns and his wife, Esther, make draperies for a living.

Because of this, bolts of drapery material tend to pile up like cordwood in their renovated attic-workroom.

Like any fine craftsman, Gunther is unnaturally proud of his profession. "Listen, it don't make no mind what kinda decoratin' you might do, me an' the missus can match your paint perfect. I mean, you won't be able to tell where paint stops and drapery starts."

Keeping all that cloth handy seems like a fine idea, except Gunther's pack-rat blood keeps whispering, "No matter how small, never throw cloth away."

"Gunther," Esther says weekly, "nobody makes windows six inches tall. Get those useless scraps outta our house."

"*Scraps?* Woman, what if we needed one of those exact pieces of material, and we didn't have it. Listen, you just never know." That has been Gunther's parting shot in every argument with Esther for going on thirty years.

But then a brushfire drove a sizable tribe of otherwise contented field mice out of a comfortable burrow and into Gunther's hoard of cloth fragments. The mice, quick studies at recognizing heaven, tunneled into the bolts and stacks like fleas into a St. Bernard.

"Gunther!," Esther screamed. "Gunther, *Gunther, GUNTHER*!!" When Gunther pulled himself panting and wild-eyed into the attic, he found Esther pointing a trembling finger at a mound of fluffy threads. "Mice! Mice! Mice! Mice!" was all she could gasp.

Gunther grabbed a roll of blue brocade, but a nest of baby mice, looking forever like pencil erasers, fell out and began crawling toward Esther. She screamed, clawed her way out the dormer window, and slid down their sycamore tree.

"Get the mousetrap!" Gunther yelled at his skinned and ragged wife.

"Get it yourself! I'm not coming near that room for the rest of my life."

"Forget it. There's too many for traps." Gunther kicked at one scurrying mouse, then threw a book at another climbing a bolt of metallic weave.

Gunther figured a mouse in its natural habitat was probably good ecology, but in this particular case, his private stock had been invaded, his wife was out the price of some Wal-Mart pantyhose and a double-knit power-suit she got at a garage sale, and he was missing "Nashville on the Road." A man can only stand so much. "Somebody gimme a stick!" he yelled.

Unfortunately, the first thing to hand was a hoe handle Esther used for turning drapery hems. He flailed away at the bolts of cloth until dust motes swirled in a fog. Suddenly, the granddaddy of all West Texas mice zipped across a windowsill.

"Gotcha, you miserable . . ." he snarled as he poked at the gray blur. When the mouse skittered across the dresser, Gunther slashed down with the hoe handle, missing the mouse but shattering Esther's antique mirror.

"Saw outta there, you meddlesome . . ." Gunther lunged back and forth across the cluttered room like a love-crazed buffalo, battering furniture, smashing coffee cups, and thoroughly terrorizing the one-ounce furball.

Finally, he cornered the mouse next to the stairwell. With one enormous grunt, Gunther's dented hoe handle lashed downward just as his foot skidded on a throw rug.

"Oh, I got the mouse all right," Gunther explained. "Couldn'ta hit him straighter. But when I skidded, the hoe handle kept swinging, and the next thing I knew, hoe handle, mouse, and might near an acre of plaster was down inside the wall of our stairwell."

Of course, by this time the mouse was about an eighth of an inch thick and dead as a bootheel, but he was also totally out of reach somewhere in the vicinity of the house's foundation. That didn't bother either Gunther or Esther—for about forty-eight hours. Then the mouse wreaked his olfactory revenge.

"I don't know the chemical analysis of your average mouse, but it must be terrifyin'. Listen, I shot a skunk under our brooder house, but that was lilac-water compared to that dead mouse."

"Where y'all stayin' now, Gunther?"

"In that campin' trailer of Ambrosio's." He shook his head. "I don't know, I may have to burn that house. You been downwind of my place lately?"

"What about your scraps?"

"Aw, *those* I saved! There's some really good pieces there. The cleaner made me a group price." He sipped his coffee. "Listen, when it comes to fine fabric, you just never know."

Back-Room Marauder

We had an interesting morning here in Cedar Gap a few days ago. Noisy—but interesting.

It started about breakfast-time in the Palace Cafe. A dozen or so people sat wallowing into the day when Deputy Sheriff Donnie Sue Kingsbury walked in.

"Hey, Donnie Sue," somebody yelled, "arrested any animals lately?"

She started to explain why she gave Calvin Kinchlow's myopic old bluetick hound a jaywalking citation for bolting right into the path of her police cruiser, causing her to level three pecan saplings and Calvin's mailbox. Suddenly, a scream echoed out of the back storage room of the cafe. Brenda Beth Kollwood bolted through the door and out into the cafe.

"There's something alive in there!" Brenda Beth shouted.

"Probably a mutant from the bottom of IdaLou's grease can," Yancy McWhirter muttered, turning back to his coffee.

Donnie Sue frowned as she unsnapped the button on her chromed .44 Magnum. Her theory runs that nothing clears up a perplexing quandary like staring into a howitzer-sized gun barrel. "Ever'body down!" Donnie Sue yelled.

"Somebody go get Edgar Allen over here!" Yancy whispered. "He's gettin' his toupee restyled over at the Fontainebleau . . . never mind, he heard the scream."

Edgar Allen Plymate, the peace justice from down at Winters, jiggled through the door, his potbelly heaving from the fifty-yard run. "I thought I heard—" Then he stopped, panting. "Donnie Sue! Now, babe, we've talked about this sorta thing before."

"Shut up, E. A. Brenda Beth says there's somethin' in that store-room, and I'm—" At that instant, something shattered several bottles of unnamed liquids. "That's it. I'm goin' in!"

"Now, Donnie Sue," Edgar Allen whispered, licking his lips. "That might be a man in there, and—"

"Then, for sure, he's gonna wish he'd called ahead," Donnie Sue muttered through gritted teeth. "Git outta my way, E. A." She grabbed her .44 in both hands and rammed the door with her shoulder. Unfortunately, it was unlocked.

Donnie Sue lurched past the swinging door into the black cavern cluttered with stacks of boxes, brooms, and shelves of half-empty jugs.

"Awright, whoever or whatever's in here has exactly five seconds to come . . . EEEEAAAAAAAAAAAAAAH! GIT AWAY FROM ME, YOU SLIMY . . ." Her squeal drowned in six thundering blasts from her .44.

Donnie Sue's guttural yells mixed with the sound of breaking glass and slammed boxes. Blue smoke and dust boiled out of the dark room. The Palace Cafe breakfast bunch dove for cover. Then, complete silence.

Edgar Allen Plymate bent over the counter, his eyes pinpoints. "Donnie Sue? Sugar, you okay?" he whispered. "Honey, talk to me! *Donnie Sue!*"

Terrified eyes peered from behind overturned tables. Slowly, the storeroom door opened. Donnie Sue stomped through, green scum sliding down her uniform, her scowling face covered with what appeared to be huge gobs of coagulated blood. Everybody screamed. Two women threw up. Edgar Allen fainted into a plate of soggy pancakes.

"I wanta know RIGHT NOW," Donnie Sue yelled through clenched teeth, "who let this snake loose?" She reached down with a small rake and lifted the two halves of a huge bull snake.

Finally Yancy got his breath. "Donnie Sue, you okay?"

"Yeah," she yelled. "This green gook is just spinach, and the red tastes like picante sauce. When I saw that snake, I just started blasting, an' I musta hit a bottle or two."

The "bottle or two" estimation missed on the low side. One of the six slugs slammed lengthwise down a shelf of creamed spinach, exploding bottles like slimy hand grenades. A gallon of industrial-strength jalapeño sauce coated the walls.

Suddenly, IdaLou Vanderburg, the main Palace Cafe cook, bolted through the front door. "Did anybody see a cardboard box with—" She stopped, abruptly aware of the multicolored police officer.

Slowly, Donnie Sue lifted the snake-on-a-rake. "IdaLou, you wouldn't by any chance be missin' one former snake, would you?"

"Ah boy!" IdaLou sighed. "Milo won't like this. Naw, sir, not at all."

It seems IdaLou spotted a mouse in the Palace Cafe, so Milo Shively loaned her his pet bull snake he kept out at his little two-bit farm to control gophers and rats. But the snake escaped from its cardboard motel.

Donnie Sue shrugged. "Coulda been worse. Coulda been Milo." She frowned. "Wonder what he'd look like on a rake, covered with spinach and picante sauce?"

"Better'n the snake," Yancy said. "But not as good as you."

Donnie Sue just grinned and reloaded.

SATURDAY'S JOURNAL

IT'S A REAL MAN'S WORLD

e know it's Saturday in Cedar Gap when Arnold Curnutt begins his weekly gripe session down at the Feed and Lumber about the wildlife that's giving him fits. Arn and his wife, Dodie, farm and ranch two sections of sorry brush country across the valley west of town, which is where Arn bumps up against all of that wildlife he hates so much.

"I just purely don't know what I'm gonna do about that ol' boar possum that keeps stealin' my chicken mash. I guarantee if I ever get him in the sights of my deer rifle, he'll be the late lamented possum."

Every Saturday, we get more breathless information about some killer bobcat or pack of coyotes or maverick buck that Arn managed to kill or drive off. "I'da had a fine garden this year, except for that buncha—yeah, Ornell, lemme have an extry salt block . . . for my ol' cow—mangy deer that tromped ever' last stalk of corn in my patch."

"Was that four sacks of goat food you wanted?" Ornell Whapple, the owner of the Cedar Gap Feed and Lumber, leaned on a post and picked his teeth while a young assistant did the heavy work.

"Yeah, an' make it your best. My, uh, old nanny deserves it."

To keep their place as voting members of the club, there are certain phrases men are forced to use in bars, barber shops, and feed stores, and these phrases usually center on maiming or terrifying something. Arn has perfected every expression down to the last pushed vowel and gritted consonant.

"I had to drive clean down into that bar ditch by Sybil Jorgenson's barn to run over that ol' granddaddy skunk." Or, "I'd poison ever' last one a them coons, but it's too big a danger to my fine bird dogs."

That was a curious statement, since from the standpoint of energy, Arn's bird dogs compare unfavorably with granite. A crippled quail once outran his retriever on flat ground.

"Naw, sir, the only thing I'm sorry for now is that the deer season's over. I shoulda shot ever last one a them sorry animals. They ain't no way I'm gonna have any kinda crop, what with deer an' skunks, an' then those wildcats that keep comin' in from Mexico. I'm gonna get me one a them night scopes an' shoot about a pickup full of chicken-killin' bobcats. You know what I mean, don'tcha? An honest man cain't make a livin' no more."

That's the general tenor of conversation in a feed store, and Arn Curnutt's a master of the genre. To hear him, he'd shoot anything that can't say "How y'all doin'?"

Some of us wandered into the Palace Hotel and Cafe for our normal midmorning caffein fix. Dodie Curnutt, Arn's wife, sat nursing a cup of hot chocolate.

"Hey, Dodie," Leonard Ply said, "listen, I sure am sorry to hear about your trouble with all the coons and deer out on your place. They can be a real trial."

Dodie just smirked, nodded, and took another drink of hot chocolate.

"Right," Milo Shively said. "Ya know, I'd be glad to help hunt them some night, if Arn don't totally eradicate all of 'em first."

"I appreciate that, Milo. I'll remind Arnold." She faked a coughing fit to hide her smile.

When the rest of the men left, I sidled over. "Did I miss something, or were you laughing at Leonard and Milo?"

"Oh, my, no! I was just laughing at their concern for the wildlife on our ranch."

"You mean, it's gotten that bad?"

Dodie glanced around carefully. "Look, in this town, a man's got to keep up appearances, and being a tad bloodthirsty goes with the territory." She wrinkled her face and grinned. "Did Arnold buy a salt block today?"

"Yeah. For his old cow."

"He doesn't have a cow, old or young. The salt's for the deer on our back section."

"But Arn said . . ."

"I can figure what he said. Did he get some goat food?"

"Yeah."

"It's for a family of baby coons that lost its mama in a trap."

"And the bobcats?"

"He leaves chicken gizzards for them." Dodie sighed as she stood. "Listen, don't tell Arnold what I said. If the boys knew he truly liked those animals, it'd put dents all over his macho."

That was an easily kept secret. Not only would telling it irritate Arn, but would turn feedstore conversation into pure skimmed milk for the next decade.

Now, *that's* a truly terrifying thought.

EPILOGUE

MIND-SET IN THE GAP

edar Gap is just off the main highway
south out of Abilene, huddled up close to
the Callahan Divide—a low, flat mesa with
very little to recommend it other than the
fact that it has a gap in it that's covered
with mountain cedar.

The small town of seventy-two families
with 256 total people started back in the
1880s as a way station on a stage line. It once made it up to eighty-
six families, right after the Big War (the second one), but in '52, the
new highway cut them off and left the whole town at the end of a
county road. From that time, the town froze in size.

There are three east-west streets, Main Street (which more or less
dead-ends up against the Callahan Divide) in the middle, with North
Street and South Street in the appropriate places. Two north-south
cross streets are named after the early Texas heroes Sam Houston
and Davy Crockett.

Cedar Gap is primarily organized around agriculture, although
a few people work in Abilene or out in the county at various jobs.
It's a fine, quiet community with a handful of essential businesses

serving logical, honest, inventive, tolerant folks who've learned to muddle through their problems. You'd like to sit down with them in the Palace Cafe and have a cup of coffee.

There aren't enough places like Cedar Gap in the world.